ROOTFINGERS

ROOTFINGERS

S. ALESSANDRO MARTINEZ

NEW YORK   LOS ANGELES

Jacket design by Rejenne Pavon
Jacket Copyright 2025 by Winding Road Stories
Interior book design by A Raven Design
ISBN#: 978-1-960724-46-5 (pbk)
ISBN#: 978-1-960724-47-2 (ebook)

Published by Winding Road Stories
www.windingroadstories.com

For the Illumined Lady

PROLOGUE

AT DAMNATION'S GATE

EXCERPT: "THE LOST ART OF: ISIDORO CERVANTES"
BY CARA ANDREWS

— BRUSHMARKS MAGAZINE ISSUE 154, FEB 1995

Though Cervantes never did achieve the great level of fame and success he no doubt strove for his entire life. During the latter half of the 1920s, when his career seemed to be finally gaining steam—rising popularity, favorable writeups by critics—Isidoro Cervantes abruptly steered his artwork in a new and unexpected direction. Turning away from his customary Impressionistic repertoire of brightly-colored still lifes, sunny beach scenes, and joyful townscapes in various locations around his native Spain, Cervantes took a hard left into darker, surprisingly morbid territory, all the while incorporating a new Baroque style.

No one knows for certain why the painter forsook the

subject matter that was beginning to earn him money and a name in the art world. Some art historians speculate that Isidoro had grown increasingly bored and disillusioned with his own predictable work. That he was painting for his critics and clients instead of painting for himself. Meanwhile, others say that his new macabre direction had been his intention all along. As art historian Ezra Amon says, "Isidoro didn't plan on creating such mundane works his whole life. He had a vision. First, he needed to get his name out there in front of the public. To get his foot in the door, so to speak. Only then could he create what he truly wanted—these dark and monstrous idea that he put to canvas—and have an audience who would be willing to look."

From the few surviving letters of correspondence written by his wife Luciana to her family, friends, and other close acquaintances, there is some implication that Isidoro Cervantes may have suffered from an undiagnosed mental illness at this point in his life, which probably would have been overlooked due to the somewhat limited understanding of such disorders during the time period. Such a thing would have likely been attributed to the fact that he was an artist, as they were often known and celebrated among their circles for their quirks, eccentricities, and peculiarities. Something we still see today with our modern celebrities and their fans.

Whatever the reason, in 1928, Cervantes, in a move that surprised the entire art scene of Los Angeles, dragged his wife and children away from the ritz, glamour, and spotlight of the California city to the small, nowhere town of Altar Hill, Kansas. Here, Cervantes began painting his infamous scenes of what can only be described as demonic creatures, nightmarish architecture, dread-inducing hellscapes, and "the kind of horrors that lurked in the darkness between the stars," as Luciana Cervantes once put it. Things that would have kept even Bosch, Salvator Rosa, and Bruegel the Elder awake at night, afraid to close their eyes.

In several letters written to her friends back in Los Angeles, Luciana Cervantes stated that her husband was "no longer the man I loved and had married," as his joyful passion for art had turned into an unhealthy obsession with creating such morbid and depraved images, each more blasphemous than the last. In 1931 Luciana left Isidoro, taking both of their sons and moving back to the city of Los Angeles. When asked what her husband's reaction was to this separation, Luciana said, "I doubt he even noticed our departure." A truly depressing statement.

For the next few years, Isidoro Cervantes would seldom be seen outside of his home in the tiny town of Altar Hill, Kansas. On the rare occasions he was spotted out and about —sometimes wandering the local park, or ambling around the gravestones of the Altar Hill Cemetery—residents reported that Cervantes looked haggard, unkempt, emaciated, and as one firsthand account states, "like the man hadn't had a proper night's sleep in months." Attempts to speak with Isidoro on these occasions was said to often result in the painter rambling almost frantically about the absolute necessity to create better and better artwork. Groceries and art supplies would be delivered to the house on a regular basis, although no one was ever permitted past the front door, and thus there is no record of whatever new artwork Isidoro Cervantes was supposedly creating within those lonely walls. Many of the townsfolk doubted the man was creating anything at all, and simply living an isolated, aimless life, having lost his muse.

In May of 1934, several citizens as well as town leadership became concerned that Isidoro Cervantes was physically and/or mentally deteriorating, and arranged for a specialist to be called in. On the night of May 25th, the day before the doctor was to arrive, neighbors reported hearing screaming and gunshots coming from the Cervantes house. Police were called to the scene. When they arrived, the officers found that all the doors were locked, and all the windows were fastened shut. After forcing their way inside, police found Isidoro Cervantes sprawled on the floor in the basement. The artist was pronounced dead at the scene.

The death of Isidoro Cervantes was officially ruled a suicide, but details of the incident including the cause of death, were never publicly released. However, an unidentified person working on the case apparently let slip that all six chambers of the revolver clutched in the hand of the deceased had been discharged, the spent casings laying on the ground near the body. Three bullets were found lodged in the living room ceiling, but the three remaining bullets were not found anywhere else in the house or in the surrounding area, nor were their points of impact.

Luciana Cervantes inherited the house from her estranged husband upon his death. She briefly visited the home to retrieve some personal property and to arrange to have the house boarded up to protect it from thieves or morbid souvenir hunters. At her only press conference on the matter, a pale and visibly-shaken Luciana begged for privacy for her sons and herself so that they may grieve in peace. She also declared that no paintings or anything else of artistic value was found inside the house before she returned to Los Angeles.

The property later passed to the elder Cervantes son who finally sold it earlier this year to a house flipping company. Representatives of the company have stated that they were the first to enter the house since Luciana had it sealed. They had most certainly hoped to find valuable artworks inside, but were apparently disappointed.

Such a tragic ending. Who knows what sort of impact Isidoro Cervantes would have had on the artistic world had his life followed a different path?

What was his true cause of death? And are there lost paintings still hidden somewhere inside that house? We may never know.

1

THE GREAT RED FIEND AND THE GIRL CLOTHED WITH THE SUN

The house around her settled into its foundations with a creaking pop.

Wren opened her eyes to a dense, enveloping blackness dotted by barely visible motes of color and small flashes of light. Blinking several times to moisten her eyeballs, heavy from the deep sleep she had just awoken from, Wren noted how in the dark of the night, her room looked no different than the backs of her eyelids.

A long inhalation filled her chest until she could breathe in no more. She then let it loose, slow and steady, until her lungs emptied. Her head swiveled from right to left, her eyes trying to discern whatever they could among the thick shadows that coated every inch of her bedroom. But it was as if the walls and furniture had been slathered in light-devouring paint. Despite many of her clothes and toys strewn across the floor, all she could make out were the merest hints of amorphous shapes that bore no resemblance to anything that was there in the daylight. Could that silhouette be her half-finished Lego castle? Or a spindly hand reaching upward? Could that massive lump be her beanbag chair piled with the books she and her grandma had borrowed from the library? Or someone sitting, silent and watching her sleep?

A shudder shook her body.

This house was dark. It was the first thing Wren had noticed after Mom and Dad had tucked her into bed on their first night here. The houses in this new town were farther apart than the neighborhood she was used to, where the homes were so close together, you could reach out a window a touch the neighbor's outside wall. And this street lacked any streetlamps until way down at the corner for some reason that Wren couldn't figure. Maybe whoever had built these streets had run out of money for more lights? Or maybe darkness just always had a way of finding itself a home, no matter what.

Wren scratched the side of her head as she passed her dry tongue over her parched lips. A glass of water would have been nice at that moment. She heard a dull plinking at the window. It looked like the rainstorm that had churned in the sky earlier that afternoon still hadn't let up. It wasn't a huge downpour at the moment, but it was coming down hard enough to produce a ceaseless, rhythmic tapping on the roof and sides of the house.

A yawn snuck out of Wren's mouth which turned into a second, bigger yawn. But a jolt of anxiety told her to keep quiet, and she snapped her jaw shut, pushing the air out of her nose instead.

There was something about being inside this house that made Wren uncomfortable at times, though after three months here she still hadn't been able to put her finger on what exactly that something was. An unease that seemed to emanate from the very walls, like sweat dripping from pores, leaking out and instilling everything it touched with its repugnant and offending odor. She often tried to convince herself that the "something" was the ever-present friction between her parents. But no, that wasn't something new. That had been present at their old home as well. This particularly unnerving feeling was unique to this new house.

Whatever it was, it was too vague to define in precise words. And now that she thought about it, Wren realized that feeling was stronger than ever tonight, almost as if the very air around her had gained tangible substance and now weighed down on her body. It could be the rain making her feel that way, she supposed. The TV weatherlady always talked about atmosphere and pressure and other science things.

Wren's shoulders made a satisfying pop as she stretched her arms over her head. She propped herself up on one elbow and squinted at the ticking clock on her nightstand with its faintly glow-in-the-dark hands and numbers. Dad had been teaching her how to tell time on these old types of clocks. She didn't understand the need for them anymore when digital clocks showed bright, easy-to-read numbers instead of these "row-min" numeral ones in a circle. Wren strained her eyes against the gloom to count the clock's lines —she wished her parents would buy her a new nightlight already after the old one had gotten broken during the move —starting from the XII that her dad said was a 12 down to where the short hand stopped, and then again for the long hand.

"2:50," she started to say out loud before the words were overtaken by yet another, louder yawn.

At the sound of Wren's voice, Churro pricked up his ears, then raised his head and looked over at her from where he lay, nestled at the end of her bed. Her family's Red Fox

Labrador lay on a pile of her blankets like some sort of cozy nest. Churro's superpower, Wren thought, was the ability to somehow steal all of the blankets without waking her up and then look adorable and innocent when confronted with his crime of thievery.

While trying to pull everything out from under the dog—Churro watching with curiosity and did not help her in the slightest—Wren realized what had awakened her. It hadn't just been the rain or the vague and unidentifiable feeling of unease. A swelling ache in her abdomen demanded release.

She groaned in irritation as she had no desire to leave her bed, even for such a quick trip. The bed was warm and comfy. Plus, this house was...well, it was still unfamiliar. Even after three months, Wren still didn't feel at home here. She wondered if she ever would. No, it was more like she and her family had been staying as guests in someone else's house. And they had worn out their welcome some time ago.

Likewise, her parents didn't seem any happier here than they had been at their old home. Well, no, that wasn't completely true. Her dad still seemed unhappy, but her mom obviously adored the new house. Still, Wren could still hear the spitting, whispered arguments coming from her parents' bedroom almost every night. She knew her mom and dad thought she was oblivious to the strain and discord; that they could "act normal" and cover up any hint of animosity between them. But Wren knew.

An undercurrent of tension had permeated their old house, snaking its way through the hallways and rooms, seeping into everything it touched like a deadly, infectious mold. Three months in the new house and already that same tension had infested every inch of it.

The warm pressure in Wren's bladder worsened. There was no delaying the inevitable.

Although her body protested the whole way, Wren managed to slide her legs over the edge of the bed. Her probing toes were unable to locate her fuzzy blue slippers. It never made sense to her how things could be set down in one spot and wind up somewhere else when no one had touched them. With a sigh, she slid off the mattress, Churro grumbling at all the movement that disturbed his beauty sleep. The hardwood floor was chilly against Wren's feet.

Despite the late hour and the drowsiness that tempted her back to the welcoming embrace of her soft pillow, Wren was actually glad she had woken up. If she wet the bed yet again, Mom would be super angry, and Dad would be disappointed (which was somehow worse than angry). Besides, she knew second-graders shouldn't still be bedwetters. If any of her classmates ever found out, she would die of embarrassment and never be able to show her face in public again.

"Stay, Churro, stay," she said, raising her palm toward the dog as he started to get up to accompany her. He always had to follow her wherever she went, as if letting her out of his sight would cost him his job as the family pet. "I'll be right back, Churro. Okay? Just stay and keep the blankets warm for me."

Churro settled back down, laying his head on his paws and giving a chuff of disapproval. His ears stayed up, turning this way and that, scanning for anything that might need investigation. Wren couldn't see the dog's eyes in the darkness, but she knew they were laser focused on her, following her every movement as she crossed the room, Churro's expressive little eyebrows dancing along with them.

The hinges whined a little as Wren pulled her bedroom door all the way open. She stepped over the threshold and out into the lightless upstairs hall. Her eyes had adjusted to the darkness as best they could by now, but she could still only make out blurry dark forms around her. There wasn't much furniture here, so she knew what the dark, indistinct shapes must be: the banister and stairs right in front of her, a small, three-legged table that held a ceramic table lamp nearby, the rectangular outline of a bookcase over against the wall that held all of her dad's military sci-fi novels as well as her grandma's little cherub figurines whose fake painted smiles always gave her the heebie-jeebies.

Those flashes and splotches of color continued to dance in front of her eyes. Wren often tried to make out shapes and patterns in them as she lay in bed, staring at the black ceiling, waiting to fall asleep. But this night, here in the hallway, she wished they would go away. The manner in which they seemed to skitter like bugs within the darkest corners of the walls caused goosebumps to break out over her arms and legs.

With a glance down the hall to her right, Wren could just make out the door to her parents' bedroom standing halfway open—dark gray surrounding an utterly pitch-black portal. She shivered. Unable to see anything inside her parents' room, the half-open door looked like a hole or vortex that she could somehow trip into, falling forever down into a bottomless void.

Wren turned away and headed down the hall in the opposite direction toward the bathroom. Grandma Manuela's room was right next to Wren's. Despite her incredibly loud snoring, Grandma Manuela was a light sleeper, and as Wren crept past her open doorway, she made sure to step as quietly as she could. She didn't know why she felt that it was imperative to be so silent at the moment. While she would never want to unintentionally wake her grandma, she knew even if she did, it wasn't like Grandma

Manuela would be angry at her. In fact, Wren couldn't think of a single instance of her grandma getting mad at her.

But something in the house tonight....

A floorboard groaned under Wren's foot and she froze mid-step, as if the noise might summon something evil, something dark, something not of this world, to come get her.

2

SUPERSTITION

Why was she so scared all of a sudden? Most little kids were afraid of the dark, and Wren admitted to herself that she was one of them. But her fear of the dark wasn't a debilitating, petrifying fear like a lot of other children had. The type where they would hide under the covers at the slightest noise and not move until morning. A chicken Wren was definitely not. No way. She didn't mind walking about at night if she needed to, even if it was in a strange and unfamiliar house that she had not wanted to move to. There was nothing to it. No, she didn't mind. Not that she would ever just go for a midnight jaunt just for the fun of it, though. That was silly.

In that moment, vivid images of decaying ghosts and rotting skeletons lurking in the darkness around her popped into her mind. Why did she have to think about that stuff right now? Maybe she shouldn't have snuck downstairs the other night when Dad and Grandma Manuela were watching that horror movie. The one that had starred Marty from Back to the Future in it. In the movie, Marty had been able to see ghosts and evil grim reapers that killed people and—

Stop it, she told herself. *Ghosts aren't real. And being scared of skeletons is dumb. Everyone has a skeleton inside them.*

Unfortunately, that thought made her more uncomfortable, and Wren shook it out of her head. Through the open doorway, Grandma Manuela suddenly went quiet. The silence went on and on for an uncomfortable amount of time until what seemed like hours later, Wren finally heard her grandma shift around on the creaking mattress and begin snoring once more.

Taking her chances that there weren't any killer phantoms hiding somewhere in the house waiting to grab her, Wren sprinted the rest of the way to the bathroom. Once inside, she swung the door closed as fast as she could, but stopped it before it slammed shut all the way, instead carefully twisting the glass knob and easing the whole thing into position until the latch clicked softly into place.

She stood there, silent and immobile for a second or two, then let out a long exhalation before reaching up to flip on the lights. The sudden, blinding illumination stung her eyes, and for a split second, she expected to see the hooded reaper from the movie—*The Frighteners*, that's what it had been called—standing before her, revealed by the harsh overhead bulbs. But, of course, there was nothing there waiting to cleave her in two with its scythe and spirit her soul away.

Stop being a chicken, she ordered herself and headed for the toilet. She lifted the lid all the way up, but lost her grip on it before setting it in place. With a gasp, and quick reflexes, she managed to catch the thing before it could slam itself down with a loud crash. Her heart beat its fists against the inside of her ribcage.

Stupid.

After peeing, Wren tossed her toilet paper into the bowl, reached for the handle, hesitated a moment, then flushed. She gritted her teeth. It was the loudest sound in the world at that moment; the surge of water, the rattling of pipes, the gurgle-plop of everything being sucked down.

Just hurry up already.

A little plastic stepstool with a cartoon giraffe on it was kept under the sink for Wren's use. She pulled it out and stepped up onto to it, gazing at herself in the mirror. She retracted her lips and examined the fresh red gap in the bottom row of her teeth. She had lost the tooth just this week at school as she was eating her peanut butter sandwich during lunch. Her tongue poked through the gap like a worm as she continued to grin at herself in the mirror.

An unexpected chill ran through her just then and her mouth snapped shut. Probably just her body reminding her to get back to the comfort of her bed. Wren turned the faucet on, and as the frigid water cascaded over her fingers, she imagined rushing back to bed, diving under the covers, and sticking her toes under Churro's butt where it would be nice and warm. That dog was like a hairy oven, giving off enough heat to cook a frozen pizza.

Wren giggled at the thought. Cupping her hands under the water, she thought about taking a drink. She didn't feel like going all the way downstairs to the kitchen for a glass of water, and her lips and tongue were so dry. Her mouth must have been open while she slept, probably snoring like Grandma Manuela. Another giggle as she put her cupped hands to her lips and took a sip of water. It tasted like metal pipes.

"So verrry pretty," a voice whispered behind her.

3

HOUSE OF SHADOWS

The water spluttered out of her mouth, and Wren almost slipped off the stepstool as she whirled around, coming face to face with...absolutely nothing.

Someone had just spoken to her. It hadn't been a hallucination, right? She had definitely heard a voice. Could she still be dreaming? She thrust a hand under the faucet again. Icy water splashed her skin, chilling her palm and fingers. That felt real enough. She turned off the faucet. Her eyes then jumped around, flicking to every nook and cranny they could find in the bathroom: under the toilet tank, behind the hamper, up where the ugly brown tile of the walls met the ceiling.

No one. Although she hadn't pulled back the shower curtain to look in the tub. Anyone could be hiding there. Why did her mom insist on drawing the stupid thing closed instead of leaving it open when not in use?

Unsure whether or not she wanted an answer, she said, "Is someone in there?"

Or she thought she had said, but then realized no sound

had escaped her lips. Her mouth felt drier than when she had first gotten up.

Wiping her hands on her pajama pants, which were covered in smiling suns wearing sunglasses, Wren hopped off the stool and approached the tub. She reached for the shower curtain, fingers outstretched and inching their way through the air at a sloth's pace. In the back if her mind, Wren hoped a grown-up would materialize out of thin air, grab her hand, and tell her not to look.

But no such thing happened. And when her fingertips brushed the hanging plastic, she gripped a handful of the curtain and ripped it aside, revealing the tub in all its empty glory. A sigh of relief would have escaped her lips at that moment if she hadn't caught movement out of the corner of her eye. Wren's gaze snapped to the tub's drain, where something dark and sinuous poked out momentarily before slithering back inside.

A gulp forced itself through Wren's constricted throat. Could there be a snake inside the plumbing? Well, it wasn't her job to find out. She'd leave that for an adult. Wren drew the shower curtain closed again, its metal rings scraping along the support rod above. If whatever it was popped out of the drain again and couldn't see her, it would leave her alone. The logic was sound.

The creak of a floorboard right outside the bathroom caught Wren's attention, and she spun around. A light must be on in the hallway because she could see a dim glow reaching in from under the door instead of the strip of blackness that had been there minutes prior.

Maybe Grandma Manuela had gotten up, needing to use the bathroom as well?

"Grandma, are you out there?"

No answer.

Wren's heart thumped in her chest. She didn't know why.

There could be no one in the house beside her family, and it was silly to be scared of them. It's not like she was doing anything bad.

Getting down on her hands and knees, Wren lowered her body and rested the side of her head against the cool linoleum of the floor so that she could peer through the gap underneath the door. There wasn't much to see except a few inches of hardwood flooring outside the bathroom.

The lamp in the hallway had definitely been switched on, though, and she hadn't been the one who had done it. So somebody other than her had to be awake.

Just then, a thin shadow moved across the very edge of Wren's vision.

Her heart seemed to skip a beat at that moment, and Wren almost let out a yelp, but she managed to control herself. If it wasn't her grandma, then it was probably her mom. Mom often liked to work late into the night. How late, Wren never knew since her own bedtime was at 8:30 every evening. But Mom enjoyed talking about how inspiration often struck her in the dead of night when everyone else was fast asleep, and when that happened, she had no choice but to hurry downstairs to her art space in the basement and create whatever her muse was demanding of her in that moment of creativity.

Her mother was an artist and that was pretty much the entire reason Wren and her family had uprooted their whole lives and moved into this place. This house used to be owned by a painter nobody but her mother seemed to have heard of—a man named Isidoro Cervantes. It was an interesting name, Wren had to admit, and that was most likely the reason it had stuck in her mind. Other than his name, however, Wren only knew a few things about this guy. Number one, he had lived in this house a long, long time ago. Super long, like a hundred years ago or something. Number two, Mom was a *huge* fan of his art. Maybe the only fan of his art in the whole world. And number three, Wren *loathed* his art. She knew her dad didn't care for Isidoro Cervantes's artwork either. There was no doubt about that, as she had overheard him say so many a time in hushed arguments with her mom. To be fair, Dad had still agreed to move into this house because Mom wanted to. That meant he loved her very much, at least that's what Grandma Manuela said.

Wren suspected that Grandma Manuela also held a disliking for Isidoro Cervantes's paintings as well, but was too sweet and polite to say anything to Mom. Wren had decided to follow her grandma's example in not voicing her own opinions about this mystery man's artwork, since she would never want to hurt her mother's feelings.

Besides being a talented painter in her own right, Wren's mother had worked in art restoration before Wren was born. She had once explained it to Wren as "giving old paintings the new life they deserved, so they could be appreciated by a new generation." The very day they had moved into the house, Mom had found a large collection of Isidoro's paintings stashed in a hidden nook in the basement—almost like she had already known they were there—and began restoring them while continuing to work on her own art. The funny thing was, Wren remembered, the Cervantes paintings hadn't just yellowed over time, but they also looked like someone had splashed buckets of paint all over them willy-nilly.

"I bet his wife did this," Wren's mom had said, an ugly sneer on her face. "From everything I know about Isidoro's history, his wife was jealous of his talent and was always trying to hold him back."

"Maybe he did it himself," Wren's dad had suggested instead. "You never know. From what you told me about him, he went crazy there at the end of his life."

Wren had seen her mother shoot him a dirty look, as if the very notion were not only preposterous, but personally insulting. "He didn't go crazy, Chris. The poor man was abandoned by his family. Artists are much more in tune with our emotions. The betrayal of his wife, his muse, must have broke him."

The handful of Isidoro's works Mom had finished restoring now hung on walls around the house, and Wren thought whenever she passed by one that they had looked much better when they were covered in those layers of obscuring paint. Wren couldn't even tell what many of them were supposed to be paintings of.

The one hanging in the downstairs hallways could've possibly been a weird, dreamlike landscape with a forest of trees—weird trees that looked like they belonged to some desolate alien planet off in some haunted corner of the galaxy. Sometimes she thought she could see figures peeking from behind those trees. But only sometimes.

Another Isidoro painting that her mom had put up in the living room was a dreary scene of a medieval village, a peasant trudging through the dirt street, pulling a cart full of crooked bodies. If Wren stared hard enough at it, the paint would seem to shift like one of those magic pictures where you had to cross your eyes to see the hidden picture. And if she really strained her eyes, she could sometimes make out what she thought was an ugly, grimacing face hiding among all the details.

Now the painting in the—

No. Stop. She didn't want to think about those "pieces of art" right now. Not at this time of night.

Shifting her body and pressing her cheek harder into the floor, Wren tried to peer farther under the door, but it was no use.

"Mom?" Wren said through the door gap. "Are you out there?"

She waited there for an hour, or maybe it was only thirty seconds. Still, nobody answered.

Well, she couldn't lie here, peeking under the door all night until the sun came up.

As she made to move, something white and fluttery flew at Wren's face from underneath the door. A scream welled up in her chest at the same moment she inhaled in surprise, resulting in a choking croak that issued from her mouth as she scrambled backward onto the bathroom floor rug.

DISTURBING EXISTENCE

P aper.

It had been a piece of paper that flew at her, having been slipped underneath the door. That's all. A simple sheet of white paper.

Still, it took several long breaths to calm her thumping pulse and unclench her bunched muscles.

No one had ever slipped her a message before while she was using the bathroom. It was weird. Biting her bottom lip, Wren crawled over to the paper and plucked it from the floor before sitting herself back down in a cross-legged position several feet back from the door. The sheet was blank, but when she flipped it over, the other side contained two words written in heavy, scribbled pencil.

Wren had begun reading at an early age, and had no problem reading these two simple words.

"Imagine me," she whispered to herself. "Imagine me...."

What was this supposed to mean? The phrase held no significant meaning for her. At least none that she could think of. This had to be her mom or her dad playing some game with her. She doubted it was Grandma Manuela. What did her parents want her to imagine exactly? Which one of her family members was "me" if the word was referring to any of them? If this was some sort of prank or joke, she didn't get it at all.

Before she could ponder further on these words, another piece of paper slid in from underneath the door, gliding with a soft flutter right into Wren's lap.

With light, cautious fingers, she picked it up and turned it over. This one contained no words. Instead, there was a penciled sketch on the other side, quite skillfully drawn. It depicted Wren in the same smiley sun-print pajamas she was currently wearing, stepping through her bedroom doorway as she had done just moments earlier. The weird thing was that the perspective was from overhead, as if whoever had sketched the scene out had been looking down at her from the ceiling. Instinct caused her to look up at the ceiling here in the bathroom. The only thing she spotted was a tiny spider tucked in a corner minding its own business.

Wren looked back at the sketch, a frown creasing her brow The longer she studied the drawing, the more of her mom's style she could see in it; the method of shading using cross-hatching, the slightly exaggerated features of Wren's face, the way the background was skewed in some subtle manner. Having seen so much of it her entire life, she knew her mom's style well. Which was why it was easy for Wren to notice an influence in this drawing that was most definitely not her mother's usual style, which was strange. It was subtle, but no doubt there.

Leaning toward the door, Wren asked again, "Mom? Are you out there?"

Absolute quiet.

And then:

"No."

EVERY NIGHT INSPIRATION
VISITS US

The word resounded off the bathroom walls.

Wren's body spasmed backward as it tried to jump from where she sat on the ground, but her crossed legs simply jerked up and down. It was less that she'd heard the response to her question, and more that she'd felt the tickle of it, as if someone's warm breath had caressed her ear from behind her, leaving a dampness on her skin.

Head whipping in every direction—up, down, left right—she saw no one else in the bathroom. Her ear still tingled with the puff of air it had received, and she scratched at it with a knuckle. Wren placed a palm over her heart, feeling it bash around inside her. Her chest tightened in discomfort. Is this what adults meant when they talked about having a heart attack or a...what was that other one...a stroke? She sincerely hoped not.

Before Wren could get up off the floor, another sheet of paper slipped underneath the door toward her. She froze, anxiety welling in her stomach. Who was doing this? And why?

Someone was trying to frighten her, but Mom, Dad, and

Grandma would never do something like this. She wanted to yell at whoever was on the other side of the door to stop right now. That it wasn't funny. Then again, what was there to be so scared of? They were just pieces of paper with words and drawings. Nothing that could hurt her in any way.

Wren stared at the latest "gift" from underneath the door. Should she turn it over to see what was on the other side? A big part of her wanted her to leave it; that nothing good would come of it.

Before that part could choose otherwise, Wren stretched an arm forward and snatched up the paper. Her hands held it pressed against her chest as if they didn't want her to look at it. But she had to. She had to know what this paper offered.

She flipped the sheet over and was met with a new pencil sketch.

The drawing was of her again, only this time it showed her sitting cross-legged on the floor of the bathroom with a sheet of paper in her hands. This time, the point of view was from above the sink behind her.

A memory flashed in Wren's mind just then. Her parents had taken her camping somewhere in Washington last summer after she had finished the first grade. The name of the place eluded her, but she remembered miles of thick forest all around their campsite, and a big lake that seemed to go on forever, disappearing into the horizon. Wren loved swimming in that lake every day of their vacation, and early one morning, she insisted on going for a dip before they had even eaten breakfast. Mom kept saying they should wait a few more hours until the day got warmer. But it didn't feel like it was that cold out, and Wren was persistent. So, after lots of whining and begging, her parents relented. They waited for her to put on her swimsuit, then walked with her to the edge of the lake. They watched with big grins as she ran into the water, splashing and giggling with joy. However, those giggles very quickly turned to screams as Wren's body realized just how glacial the water's temperature was.

That was exactly how she felt in that moment, staring at the drawing she held in her shaking hands, like she had once more tumbled into that icy lake water, every bit of warmth sapped from her skin and bones, leaving her nothing but a shivering husk.

The part of her that had told her not to look at the paper now screamed at her to get out of the bathroom right that instant and run into Grandma Manuela's room and wake her up. A more compelling force wanted her to turn around to look at the sink.

That tightness in her throat had returned, and Wren made herself swallow the stone that had formed there. It didn't want to go down.

Inhale.

She got to her feet.

Exhale.

What would be standing behind her? Did she really want to know?

No, she didn't want to, Wren decided. But she had to know. Morbid curiosity demanded it.

She spun around so fast it made her dizzy for a second.

No one was there in the bathroom with her.

A line from a book Dad had read to her once, *Alice's Adventures in Wonderland,* popped into her head:

We're all mad here. I'm mad. You're mad.

Wren knew that, in that context, "mad" meant "crazy."

Was she as mad and as crazy as the inhabitants of Wonderland? No, she wasn't crazy. Being crazy meant seeing and hearing things that weren't real. Crazy people were like that man who she would often see in the park next to the school. He was always dressed in the same dirty clothes and argued for hours on end with things that no one else could see. Wren was afraid of that man, though she also felt sorry for him and wished someone would help him.

But no, she herself was not crazy.

Wait, did crazy people know they were crazy?

Her back to the door, facing the sink, Wren said, "Who's there? Why are you hiding? I know you're there." The words had come out of her before she even realized she had said them. Her voice had sounded much more confident than she felt.

Looking down at the drawing gripped in her hands, she confirmed that the artist's point of view was from just above the sink. She looked up and stared at the white porcelain basin in front of her, then lifted her gaze to the mirror she had just looked at herself in. The mirror was hinged so it could swing open to reveal the medicine cabinet set into the wall behind it where bandages, cough syrup, Aspirin, and Dad's shaving stuff was kept.

The mirror was now ajar, a thin strip of blackness separating the mirror's edge and the wall. Wren was positive the cabinet had been closed when she'd been washing her hands. Now it was open.

Mirrors didn't open themselves.

She opened that medicine cabinet at least twice a day to brush her teeth. The catches weren't loose. The mirror always stayed in place when she closed it.

Staring into that black sliver, Wren was unable to see the contents of the medicine cabinet, even though she was pretty sure the bathroom's light should have been enough to dispel any shadows inside of it. Instead, from what she could see, it looked like the mirror opened up into an endless hole that ran deep into the wall.

Wren let the paper fall from her hand where it floated to the floor with a slow, whispered rustling. Her entire focus was glued to the open medicine cabinet, for she could now hear something in there. She had no idea how houses were built. Were there spaces in between a house's walls? And if so, what was in there, if anything at all? Were they just empty spaces? Did they lead somewhere? They had to, since Wren could hear something moving about in there. Maybe they led outside? A bunch of leaves and debris from outside had probably found a hole in the house's exterior, found its way inside after being blown in by the wind, and was now accumulating in those wall spaces. Or, even more likely, some mice had made their home here. Old houses always got mice and bats and bugs. At least that's what she saw on TV. They were in the walls, scratching around looking for ways to get into the human's food.

Wren knew none of that was true. Not at all. It was a lie. Maybe it would have been true in a normal house, but not this one. This house was wrong. Deep down, she knew she was lying to herself so she wouldn't feel so scared.

But she *was* scared. More terrified than she could ever remember being. Wren's entire body buzzed with fear. All the spit had been sucked out of her mouth and throat as if with a vacuum. What felt like a horde of snakes thrashed around inside her belly.

It wasn't leaves blown by a breeze or scratching mice that were making noise.

Something much bigger was in the wall. Moving around. Moving toward her.

"Da...." Her voice refused to cooperate.

The mirror opened a little wider on noiseless hinges. There was a moment of stasis as Wren watched, the entire house took in a breath with her as she waited, frozen in place.

What looked like thin tree roots, the color of dirty beets, writhed out of that void inside the medicine cabinet. They crawled over the edge of the cabinet, anchoring themselves to the wall, little offshoots rapidly growing from the main roots as they slithered along. Wren, mesmerized, watched in both fascination and fear. Plants were not supposed to move in such a way, and certainly not so fast. Her eyes traveled back toward the open mirror, back to the roots' source. The darkness in there seemed like it had solidified.

Similar to the reflection of light in a cat's eyes, multiple spots in the darkness of the medicine cabinet peered out at her, each one winking in and out at irregular intervals. Quicker than they had spread, the roots retracted, and the mirror promptly snapped itself closed.

The medicine cabinet stood as it had minutes before, as if nothing out of the ordinary had occurred.

"Dad!" Wren screamed with all the might her lungs could produce. "Grandma! Mom!"

Spinning around with enough force to slam into the bathroom door she had been backing up against, Wren fumbled with the doorknob, her sweaty fingers sliding across its smooth surface. A cry of frustration burst from her lips before she finally managed to maintain a grip on the knob and fling the stupid door wide open. Her whole body was pulsing with the same instinctive thought: she had to get to safety. Her feet carried her over the bathroom's threshold in a flash, and she immediately collided with a large, solid object on the other side.

Bouncing off the obstacle, Wren went sprawling onto the hallway floor, banging the tip of her elbow and the edge of her knee as she came crashing down, smashing into the little table that held the lamp. The lamp swayed with the impact, eventually tumbling over the table's edge, and exploding into dozens of pieces as gravity did its job dragging the pink, ceramic body down to meet the ground.

Tears welled up in her eyes, but Wren ignored the pain and instead looked up to see what she had run into.

"Churro!" she cried out in a mixture of fear, surprise, and relief as she recognized the furry roadblock.

The dog didn't respond to his name. Instead, he kept his intense, piercing gaze fixed straight ahead of him, staring without blinking an eye. The fur on his back stood straight up like he was part porcupine. Wren sprang to her feet and stumbled over to Churro, throwing her small arms around his tensed body. She let his warmth sink into her and took comfort in his familiar smell.

The bulb of the lamp on the floor was still intact, and Wren was grateful for that. Despite a new tear, the lampshade had mostly retained its shape and now directed its cone of illumination toward the far end of the hall where the door to her parents' room was. The light cast the doorframe in stark shadows, making the scene look like a panel from a comic book. Her head turned in that direction, eyes picking out every detail they could, Wren still couldn't see what in the world Churro was so fixated on, and she was certain she wouldn't want to find out.

Hoping all the noise had woken her parents or her grandma, Wren remained motionless, listening for any sounds of stirring, but never taking her eyes away from her parents' doorway. She wanted to call out, but the thought that someone might hear her, someone other than Mom, Dad, or Grandma, caused her lips to clamp shut.

After a several oppressive seconds, she realized no one was coming to investigate the racket she had just made. It made no sense. She was sure her crash had been thunderous enough to wake the neighbors.

Not looking away from the spotlighted end of the hallway, Wren slipped her fingers underneath Churro's collar. Grandma Manuela's room was only a few feet away, her door still wide open.

"Come on, Churro," Wren urged in a harsh whisper. She

tugged on the collar, but the dog wouldn't budge from where he sat. Wrapping her arms around him again, she tried to pull the dog toward Grandma Manuela's room. "Churro, please. Come on!"

Churro let out a deep, throaty growl which rumbled throughout his whole body and up into Wren's arms. The sound shocked her, and she let go of him, appraising the dog with wide eyes. She had never heard him make such a sound before, not at the mailman or at other dogs, not even at the fat gray cat that liked prowling in their yard. Churro's threat wasn't aimed toward her, she realized. The dog still stared straight ahead. And when Wren turned to look once more at what was upsetting the him so much, she sucked in her breath in a choked gasp.

From the top of her parents' doorway, she now saw the same type of roots as the ones from the medicine cabinet growing and spreading. How was this happening? There were several large trees the surrounded the house. Had one of them mutated and started growing on the roof, sending its fibrous tendrils down into the house's structure? Over the doorframe, up the wall, and along the popcorn ceiling those roots stretched until each one was about the length of Wren's entire arm.

It made no sense. Back at their old home, she had often helped Grandma Manuela in the garden. And she did the same here at the new house. Wren knew at least the basics when it came to plants. Plants took days, weeks to grow—so slowly that it was imperceptible. In no way did they spread out instantaneously as these strange things were doing right before her eyes.

Those beet-red roots quivered like they were eager to prove just how unnatural they were. Appearing to flex their knotted, sinewy forms up on the ceiling, they moved up and down, tapping up on the ceiling. No, not tapping.

Drumming. The roots were drumming like Wren's father drummed his fingers on the table when he was bored or when her mother was yelling at him.

A disturbing notion occurred to Wren as she studied the growth up above her. She counted each of those roots as they tap-tap-tapped, little woody offshoots slowly sprouting out of each one.

There were ten main roots, five spreading to the right, and five spreading to the left.

Drum. Drum. Drum.

As Wren's mind reluctantly came to a conclusion, her fear was confirmed as half of the roots detached from the ceiling, hung in the air for a moment, then curled into a ball with one root sticking up, in the manner of a closed fist with its index finger extended.

It made a "come here" motion at her.

These weren't roots, they *were* fingers. And fingers were attached to hands. Hands were attached to arms. And arms were attached to....

The roots retracted and vanished back into her parent's bedroom in a flash.

A low rumble of a voice, sounding like it spoke through a mouthful of syrup, floated from out of the bedroom doorway.

"Wren. Wren. Wren. Wren." It possessed the cadence of a train chugging along.

"Wren, Wren, Wren, Wren." The train was gaining speed and volume.

"Wren, Wren, Wren, Wren!" Faster and faster. Louder and louder.

"Wren! Wren! Wren! Wren!" It was racing along like its brakes were out.

Then an abrupt, pulsating quiet, pressing against her eardrums, squeezing her head. The whole world had gone silent. All noise ceased to exist. She had gone deaf and so had the universe.

"WREEEEEEN!"

It was the excruciating shearing sound, somehow both deep and shrill, that she imagined a train would produce as it derailed and crashed into the hard-packed earth around its tracks.

"Churro, run!" Wren yelled and made for her grandmother's room, once again attempting to drag Churro along by his collar. The dog paid no heed to her command and broke out of her grip, the rough nylon collar burning her hand as it ripped away. Churro tore down the hall toward her parents' room, barking up a vicious storm and disappeared inside the blackness of the open door.

"Churro, no!"

Despite what she had seen and heard, Wren wasn't about to let her dog rush into danger. She made to sprint after him when something grabbed the back of her pajama top. The force dragged her backward over a threshold before a door slammed shut in front of her, muffling Churro's frantic barking.

Wren spun around in the lightless room, trying to identify her rescuer.

"Grandma?" she panted.

"Madre de Dios, what is going on out there?"

6

VISIÓN FANTASMALA

"Grandma, there's someone in the house!" Wren shouted, arms flailing.

Grandma Manuela stood there in the dark, the silhouette of her squat form adjusting the large glasses on her face. Then, with a click, the lamp on her nightstand lit up, the soft, warm glow illuminating Grandma Manuela's weathered brown face, which helped soothe Wren's fear-wracked nerves a bit. But she was still filled with an anxious energy that coursed through her body like lightning bolts

Finally, after putting her steely gray hair up into a short ponytail, her grandmother said, "Somebody is in the house? Who is in the house?"

"I-I don't know!" A bubble of anxiety and dread kept traveling up and down between Wren's belly and chest. It made her nauseated, though instead of throwing up her dinner, she vomited a flood of words. "I woke up 'cause of the rainstorm. Well, it wasn't really because of the rain, I had to go pee real bad. But-but when I was in the bathroom, there was something in there with me. I thought I saw something in the tub. Then there were these...these weird drawings that I thought maybe Mom was pushing under the door. And something was inside the medicine cabinet. Like… like roots! Weird red roots! And just now I…!"

Wren's chest tightened as it demanded she take a breath, lest she collapse. She had to make her grandma understand.

"Calm down, mija," Grandma Manuela said. She placed both hands on Wren's shoulders and sat her down on the edge of the bed. "Let's take a second to breathe. Okay, so you woke up and you think you saw roots? Like from a tree?"

"Not like regular roots! They were growing all fast in the bathroom and then in the hallway and—"

"Maybe you had a nightmare and got scared?"

"No!" Wren squeaked out, trying not to scream. "It was a monster! The roots were its fingers or something!" Her hands flapped in the air with frustration. If she flapped any harder, she'd take off, flying around the room. "Don't you hear Churro barking at it? We have to go get him!"

The only sound Wren could hear as she shut herself up and listened was the rain pattering against the house. That couldn't be. Even with the door closed, they should've been able to hear Churro's furious howling. Had something happened to her dog?

Oh, no, no no….

Or had she really imagined everything? Had a bad dream, like her grandma said, and had gone to the bathroom half asleep, images from her nightmares still dancing in front of her eyes, her brain, not able to distinguish between reality and dream, confusing itself? Sure, she'd had plenty of bad dreams before, but never a nightmare this vivid.

Grandma Manuela removed her glasses and set them on the nightstand bedside the lamp before walking over to the window that overlooked the street. She rocked back and forth on the balls of her feet as if she were pondering something. The rain kept up its steady rhythm.

Pitter-patter. Pitter-patter.

The house let out a creaking moan, and Wren nearly fell off the bed as she started. The house had just settled. That had to be it. Another creak and a loud pop resounded below the floor. A low rumbling, then the central heating came on and hot air whooshed out of the floor vents.

Wren was way too anxious and jittery for her own liking. Her dad called it that "ants in your pants" feeling. She hated that sensation, like every muscle in her body needed to be doing something or else she would burst. Before she could say anything, however, her grandma spoke.

"Your father used to be very scared of the dark when he was little too," Grandma Manuela said, still staring out the window. "I can't count the times he woke up from a nightmare and made me and your grandpa check under the bed and in the closet for monsters or ghosts or whatever else he thought was hiding under there waiting to get him." She chuckled. "Oh, the dreams he would tell us he had. Silly things. All children are afraid of the dark, mija. It is a natural thing to be afraid of, I think. When you are in the darkness, when you can't see anything, your mind knows that there could be something standing right next to you and you wouldn't even know it was there."

Wren sat on the edge of the bed, quiet, looking down at her dangling feet and wondering where her grandma was going with this. Her fingers fidgeted in her lap. She wanted to call for help. Maybe phone the police so they could deal with the intruder. Her grandma didn't have a phone in her room, though. They would either have to get to the line in her parents' room or the one in the living room.

If the whole thing had been a simple nightmare, would she get in trouble if she called the police? Or even just shouted out of the window for the neighbors?

But the whole experience had been so vivid, it couldn't have been a dream.

Looking up, Wren saw Grandma Manuela looking at her over her shoulder at her. The kindly smile that was always present on those wrinkled lips, the smile that never failed to ease whatever troubles Wren was going through at the moment, was now nowhere to be seen. There was a smile on her grandma's face all right, but it was different, off in some way. It was like a smile one would give to a stranger on the street instead of to a granddaughter.

"Come over here by the window, mija," her grandma said, gesturing for Wren to come stand beside her.

Doing as she was told, Wren slid off the bed, planting both feet firmly on the floor. She wiggled her toes and fidgeted with her fingers for a moment. She had never gone against whatever Grandma Manuela asked of her, so why was she considering it now? Because her grandma had never made Wren so uneasy before.

This whole surreal night was messing with her head, making her doubt even the most familiar of things.

Wren joined her grandmother at the window. Grandma Manuela placed an arm around her granddaughter's shoulder and went back to gazing outside. The rain plinked against the glass, little beads forging watery trails as they slipped ever downward until they were out of sight. If Wren didn't know better, she would have said the raindrops had a faint glow to them, a dull blue luminescence that shone from within their centers. But that wasn't possible. Water didn't glow. And as her grandma didn't seem to acknowledge that anything weird was going on with the rain, Wren decided it was yet another thing to chalk up to her dreamy, sleepy brain.

"Tell me," Grandma Manuela said, squeezing Wren's shoulder. "What do you see out there?"

Wren looked up at her grandma's face, then turned to peer out the window.

"Um, I don't know."

Apart from the rain, Wren realized she could see nothing beyond the fence that surrounded their yard. It was like the rest of the neighborhood—the houses, the streets, the sidewalks, and street signs—had all been swallowed up by the lonely night. Eyes travelling upward to the sky, she also saw that the moon, stars, and clouds were nowhere to be seen, only a blank, black canvas of nothingness. The unrelenting darkness of her parents' bedroom doorway. The unending void inside the medicine cabinet.

The black emptiness that she now saw outside reminded Wren of those same things and filled her with an obscure dread that the world was not just very wrong this night, but also somehow incomplete. It was missing vital pieces of itself. Wren sensed it in her bones, though she couldn't comprehend it. A sense of vertigo caused her vision to wobble. She would've stumbled backward if her grandma hadn't had an arm on her shoulders.

"It needs some more work, doesn't it?" Grandma Manuela said with a sigh. "Everyone has the ability to make their own world. But only a select few possess the necessary talent to create a masterpiece."

Wren had no idea what her grandma was talking about, and as she listened, she continued to watch the storm on the other side of the window. She was confident now that she'd been right. The rain *did* have a subtle, blue-tinted glow to it.

"Grandma, I don't think I was dreaming," Wren whispered. The arm across her shoulders suddenly felt too heavy. "There's something in the house with us, and I'm scared."

7

GREYED-HAIR RAINBOW

Grandma Manuela remained quiet a moment before clearing her throat, sounding like it was clogged with phlegm.

"Do you believe monsters live in the dark, mija?" she asked. "Do you believe there are things that hide under your bed, or in your closet, or in the corners of your vision, just waiting for their chance to get you when you aren't looking?"

This was the weirdest talk her grandma and she had ever had. Grandma Manuela's conversations usually revolved around topics such as Wren's day at school or whether she'd like some cookies when her parents weren't around to say no. Normal grandparent things.

Wren gazed about the room, trying to ground herself. Set into the far wall, a small shelf held a collection of little porcelain flowers and an old black and white photograph of Grandma Manuela and Grandpa Arturo on their wedding day. Nearby, an antique wardrobe overflowed with pastel skirts, pants, and blouses, as well as several huipil dresses in more vibrant colors, and fancier outfits reserved for church. Several small crucifixes hung above the bed right next to three framed paintings: one of the Virgin Mary standing among the clouds, one of Jesus praying in a garden, and one of a shepherd boy guiding his flock of sheep across a wide green field. At least these paintings weren't as creepy as the ones Mom hung around the house—those awful Isidoro Cervantes paintings she loved so much.

"Well?" Grandma Manuela prompted.

Wren had almost felt normal again, looking at all of her grandma's thing around the room. But then the present crashed down upon her again, demanding her undivided attention.

"I...I don't know."

Her grandma shifted from one foot to the other, the floorboards squeaking under her. "You don't know what? If you believe in monsters? Or you don't know if you believe the monsters are there in the dark waiting for you?"

Wren didn't really understand the difference or why Grandma Manuela was asking these things. She'd had enough of this weirdness

"We need to check on Mom and Dad and Churro," Wren answered instead, hoping to get her grandma to focus on what were the more urgent matters. "Whoever is in the house is in their room. I saw it."

"Of course there's someone in their room," Grandma Manuela said in a teasing voice. "Your parents are in their room. It's where they sleep."

"No!" Wren snapped. Frustration jolted inside her, but was rapidly replaced with regret at having taken such a tone with her grandmother. She bit her bottom lip until it hurt. "Someone else. A...." Her hands twisted together in her lap. "I saw a monster in there. I know I did."

"So, you do believe in monsters," her grandma replied.

Neither of them said anything for several seconds which stretched on to several discomforting minutes. Then with a thump, Grandma Manuela put her forehead to the glass of the window, humming a tune to herself—one that Wren didn't recognize. Weak moonlight finally shown from the sky, streaking downward like a faint brushstroke, although it still revealed absolutely nothing past their fence. Emptiness outside those windows, only emptiness. Endless space. The house was alone—an island floating in a never-ending abyss.

Wren shivered. Why was her grandma was acting so weird? Was she sick? This was not like her at all. In such a situation as this, Wren had would have expected her grandma to scoop her into a warm embrace filled with head kisses and reassuring sayings.

Tonight was wrong. The house was wrong. Her grandma was wrong.

"We have been here a few months now," Grandma Manuela said. "What do you think of this house? Are you all settled in now? I know moving is hard, but your father thought it was a good idea. Your mom and dad...oh how they fought. I know you heard it sometimes, but they reserved the real tongue lashings for when you weren't around. Those were fun to listen to."

Did her grandma just let out a giggle? Why was she saying these things?

"Your parents really hate each other. They think they love each other still, but they're being stupid. I see it. A blind man could see it. The only thing keeping them together these past few years has been you. But that might not be enough anymore. That's why your daddy bought this house. He wanted to appease your mother, get her to love him again. Oh, she's happy here. But it's not you or your father she loves. Art is her true love, her true passion."

"No." Wren shook her head. None of this could be true. "Just because they fight sometimes doesn't mean they don't love each other."

"Such denial." Lifting a finger, Grandma Manuela began drawing in the condensation that had gathered on the interior of the window. A wide circle appeared. That in turn became a crude frowny face with a droopy mouth and big Xs for the eyes. Grandma Manuela kept drawing, her finger squeaking every so often as her skin slid across glass, until there were four faces of varying sizes outlined on the window.

"Are you nervous, mija?" Grandma Manuela finally broke the silence.

The heavy, oppressive weight Wren had felt earlier descended upon her again. An uncomfortable tingling spread itself across her scalp, down her neck, and into her shoulders like thousands of ants marching under her skin.

When Wren didn't answer, Grandma Manuela's hand flew up, her palm slapping against the window so hard, Wren thought it might shatter. The hand slowly slid down the glass with a stuttering screech, but instead of the drawn faces simply being wiped away, a thick, dark liquid was left behind in a long, smeared handprint.

"You should be more than nervous, Wren," Grandma Manuela said, smearing more of the liquid all over the window. It was like Grandma Manuela's skin was producing the substance, her pores seeping with whatever it was.

Wren took a step backward, away from the figure at the window.

"What's fun for me, Wren, won't be fun for you." Another giggle, too deep and discordant to have come from her grandmother's vocal cords.

Grandma Manuela turned around. The soft glow of the bedside lamp only lit one side of her face, the other half caked in thick shadow. A thin string of drool seeped out from the corner of her mouth.

"Mija," The word was said in a mocking tone. "You should

definitely be more than nervous. You should be fucking terrified."

Even after everything she'd experienced so far tonight, Wren was still stunned. She had never once heard Grandma Manuela say a bad word, and the word she had just heard uttered in a voice she had known all her life was like a slap in the face that sent her mind reeling.

"You're not my grandma." It was the most confident statement Wren had made all night.

With surprising speed, the thing pretending to be Grandma Manuela lunged forward and wrapped its now-cold fingers around Wren's wrist in a painful grip. Wren cried out in a desperate attempt to shake the hand loose; a hand that no longer felt like flesh, but rather like wet, slippery dough.

"Let me go!" Wren cried out, tears streaming down her face.

Grandma Manuela's face twitched and spasmed like it was running through every emotion it knew how to make.

Then her grandma's face shifted.

In her panic-stricken state, Wren couldn't understand what she was seeing as her grandmother pushed her to the floor and loomed over her. It was like Grandma Manuela's face was drooping...melting. Her wrinkly skin oozed down from her skull as her face hovered above a shrieking Wren, who thrashed around, pinned against the unyielding floor underneath the weight of this fiendish horror masquerading as her loving grandma. Bulging eyes bubbled and then softened like runny yellow eggs to dribble down cheeks in wet globs. Saggy, dissolving lips stretched down like greasy worms eager to give Wren a slobbery kiss.

"So pretty," the monster gurgled, a red, viscous liquid pouring from out of its mouth and splattering down on Wren's face and chest. "Sooooo pretty. Shall I keep you in a glass case and watch your body rot and decay? I think I will. What wonderful colors the human corpse creates when it putrefies."

"Get off me!"

In a burst of strength, Wren managed to rip her arm out of Grandma Manuela's slimy, sticky grip, feeling beyond queasy when several wrinkled fingers came along with it, still gripping her wrist.

"Stop!" Wren screamed. Her heartbeat had ramped up to such a degree, she could barely hear anything above the hammering in her ears.

Grandma Manuela's head and body continued to melt and liquefy, covering Wren in multicolored ooze. Flailing, Wren desperately clawed at her grandma. Her small fingers sank into the brittle bone and cold sludge of Grandma Manuela's face, deeper than should have been possible.

In terrified confusion—

—*was she hurting her grandma?*—

—*this thing was* not *her grandma!*—

—Wren ripped her hand down, bringing a large chunk of Grandma Manuela's skull with it, clutched in her shaking fist. She hadn't meant to, but Wren had ripped a good portion of her grandma's head and face off. Dear God, she hadn't meant to.

"Pretty little chica," Grandma Manuela croaked, the top-left part of her head down to her jaw now just a ragged trench. Instead of blood, more multi-colored fluid gushed from out of that fresh wound as Grandma Manuela collapsed on top of Wren, melting into a thick, gooey muck on top of her.

In all of her wildest nightmares, Wren could never have thought up such a horrifying scenario as what she had just witnessed. The utter hideousness was too much for her, and she scrambled to her feet in a cold panic. She tried to wipe her liquified grandma off of her, all the while shrieking at the top of her lungs, her body sounding an alarm for every human being that it could reach, alert them to the horrendous fact that reality as they knew it was breaking down into something atrocious and unrecognizable.

After slipping several times in the viscous puddle of what had been Grandma Manuela, Wren managed to wrench the bedroom door open and flee.

8

SILENCE EVERYWHERE

After racing out of her grandmother's bedroom, Wren made for the stairs, stumbling in the darkness, but running down each one as fast as her short legs could go until her foot slipped and she came crashing down hard on her tailbone midway down the staircase.

The impact rattled her whole body, which in response, shut down in that instant, refusing to move. Her mouth hung open, her throat straining, but Wren realized she had stopped screaming. Her vocal cords were producing nothing more than a faint crackle. She wanted to keep screaming, though, to get rid of the vortex of horror that had sprung up inside her. She wanted the whole neighborhood to hear her screaming, but the screams wouldn't come anymore, so she finally shut her mouth, her jaw closing with the slowness of a rusted hinge.

She wanted Churro to come find her and lead her out of the house to safety.

Where was he? He had to be somewhere in the house. There were only so many places he could hide. Not that he would ever hide. She knew Churro would come to her rescue if he could.

Frozen on the stairs, Wren sat in silence, trying not to imagine what could prevent Churro from finding her. The light from the fallen lamp in the upstairs hallway must have gone out, because the house around her lay in inky shadow. A wave of bitter coldness crawled up her spine and down her limbs. She shivered. At that moment, Wren had no desire to move from where she sat, but she had to do something.

Had she closed the door as she escaped from her grandma's bedroom? Wren couldn't remember, but she was most definitely not going to go and check. Against her wishes, her brain conjured up the vivid imagery of her liquified grandma seeping from underneath the door, staining the hardwood as it spread in all directions.

A painful dry heave wracked her tiny frame. Wren raised her fingers to her face to wipe away the hot tears that streamed down her cheeks. That was when she recoiled after catching a whiff of her hands and the muck they were covered in. She strained her eyes in an attempt to identify the viscous substance in the dark.

Melted...she melted all over me....

The very notion that Grandma Manuela's brains and flesh coated her fingers caused her to gag several more times, her mouth salivating in preparation for the expulsion, but she managed to keep everything down. When she felt like she had control of her stomach again, Wren gave her hands a tentative sniff, then her arms, and finally the damp material of her pajama shirt.

Wait. She knew that smell. She had smelled it almost every day of her life due to her mother's line work.

"Paint?" she whispered, hoping that's what it really was. Despite how tense things had been recently between her parents, the smell of paint had always reminded her of home, and thus was a familiar comfort. But in such a context as this, Wren felt confused, frightened, and appalled. Better to be covered in paint than blood and gore. But if that's what her had pouring out of Grandma Manuela, if that's what she had melted into, what did that mean? That her grandma wasn't a human being?

That thing upstairs hadn't really been Grandma Manuela. No, no, no. It couldn't have been the kindly woman she had known all her life.

If that were the case, then what had she…it…that thing actually been?

That was a terrifying mystery that would have to wait until she was out of danger.

Something smacked against the side of the house, snapping Wren out of her thoughts. Managing to pull herself up off the step where she sat, Wren made her way down the rest of the staircase and scrambled toward the front door of the house in a haze of unreality. The oval of frosted glass set into the door showed nothing of the outside, not even the porchlights of the neighboring houses. Strange, but that didn't matter. She needed to get out of here. Outside was safer than inside right now. Whatever was happening tonight, it was all too much for her to handle on her own. The situation required adult intervention. Grown-ups knew how to fix any problem. Maybe Mom and Dad were actually outside for some reason, waiting for her to come out. If she still couldn't find the both of them, then perhaps going next door to Miss Russell's house for help would be good enough. Anything would be better than dealing with this nightmare all alone.

As she reached for the doorknob, Wren stopped herself. Her parents might be outside, but they also might not be. She knew her mother would be angry if she went out of the house at this time of night—"pissed" is what her dad would say. While they had still been getting ready to move here to the new house, Wren remembered, her dad had taken her to the theaters to see a movie. Mom hadn't wanted to come, telling them she had a lot of work to do. They had gotten home much later than expected because they had stopped afterward to get ice cream. Oh boy, her mother had been "pissed" all right. After quickly being bathed and put to bed by her silent and purse-lipped mother, Wren was unable to tune out the argument that echoed up to her bedroom from downstairs.

"What were you thinking? She's only seven. Chris. It's way past her fucking bedtime!"

"Only by an hour! She's on summer break for fuck's sake, it's not like she has to get up early for school tomorrow."

"That doesn't matter. I've said it a million times that she needs to be in bed by 8:30. She's not some little drinking buddy you can stay out all night with! Why do I have to be the one who's always laying down the rules and the discipline? You're always trying to undermine my authority to make me look like the bad guy here. I'm sick of it!"

"Come on, Rebecca, that's not fair. We went to a fucking movie and ice cream! I was just trying to cheer Wren up. She's super upset about leaving behind her school and her friends and the only home she's ever known. Maybe if you bothered to focus even a fraction of the attention on your family that you give to your art for one damn second, then maybe, just maybe, you would've noticed how lost and confused your daughter has been feeling these last few months!"

"Oh, go to hell, Chris. You know how important my art is to me. You fucking know. But that doesn't mean I neglect my family in the goddamned least! Don't you dare ever try to imply that I'm a bad parent."

"All I'm saying is that maybe you should try to put your

daughter above yourself for once. I mean, my mother has been more of a mother to Wren than you have."

This last statement had been followed by an audible slap. Even after Grandma Manuela had come in to comfort her, Wren had cried herself to sleep that night.

Reluctantly, Wren let her hand drop away from the doorknob.

Leaving the house without permission in the middle of the night was out of the question, no matter what had happened. To risk calling down her mother's wrath on herself was bad enough. However, what pressed more heavily on her mind was what if she got her dad in trouble again? In no way was she going to cause a repeat of that night.

Her friend Heather's parents had gotten divorced, and Wren had seen what that had done to Heather and her family. Wren never wanted to end up like that. No matter how much her parents argued, Wren loved them both so much. She wouldn't be able to bear it if they ever split up, especially if she ended up being the cause of it. That would break her in ways she couldn't even fathom.

What to do then?

Think, Wren, think.

A light flickered to life from behind her, producing a soft blue aura. Wren spun around. The light emanated from the living room. Someone had turned on the television. Her dad often slept on the couch after falling asleep in front of the TV. At their old house, where Wren had had to pass through the living room at night to get to their only working bathroom downstairs, she would frequently see her dad there in the wee hours of the night, eyes closed, peaceful, some weird infomercial playing on the screen with the volume almost to zero. Wren thought that it was at these times that her dad looked the most serene; those nights she found him sleeping on the couch. Maybe he slept there so frequently because Mom worked on her art so late into the night, and he didn't want to be in bed alone. Never mind the fact that he was mostly always there after he and Mom had an argument.

Weighing options, Wren decided to head into the living room. The TV's glow coated the walls and furniture in a wavering blue haze, creating a multitude of shadows which danced and undulated with every movement on screen. The unnerving details of the Isidoro Cervantes painting Mom had hung on the wall behind the TV were barely visible in the dim flickering light, yet Wren's mind immediately identified and solidified the grimacing face that she could only sometimes see among the brushstrokes.

The face stared down at her, like it wanted to open its scowling mouth and say something creepy or ominous. Wren refused to acknowledge that ugly face and surveyed the room multiple times. "Dad, are you in here? Churro?"

The sofa sat empty, however, as did the loveseat and armchair.

The fear and horror that had built up inside Wren's chest crumbled into a dense heap of profound sorrow. Even though her family's absence from this room at this moment meant nothing, she was swept up in an engulfing miasma of abandonment. Where was everyone? Perhaps the monster that she had seen, the Root Fingers thing upstairs, perhaps it had gotten her family.

And had done what with them? Monsters were monsters and not human. Therefore, they possessed inhuman motivations and desires. Maybe. How could she be certain of anything relating to monsters? It's not like they taught about monsters at school. Her parents always told that monsters weren't real, yet everything tonight showed Wren that they *were* real.

She was so confused. There was no way to guess what this Root Fingers thing wanted.

Did it just want to kill them all?

Death wasn't a subject she thought about much. Wren knew that when a person died, they never came back. She had no clue where their consciousness or their soul went, but she was aware that if they did go somewhere—and not just cease to exist—then it was some place where the people who were still alive could not see them or be with them. That meant if her family had been killed by this monster, she would never see them again. Ever.

Unless it killed her as well. Took her life for its unknowable goal.

Wren shivered at the idea. She didn't want to think about this anymore. She didn't want to think about anything. At that moment, what Wren wanted the most was to be cuddled up on the couch with Mom, Dad, Grandma, and Churro, where she could close her eyes and go back to the blissful, terror-free world she had been in before waking up tonight.

Moving over to the phone that sat on the side table next to the armchair, Wren stretched out her arm and picked up the receiver, placing it against her ear. The sticky grandma-paint-gunk that covered her hands left tacky prints on the white plastic.

There was no dial tone that she could hear. Her fingers tapped several buttons on the phone's base, leaving behind more smudges and fingerprints of paint, But still, she heard nothing through at all. Wren hung up, waited a few seconds, then quickly grabbed the receiver again, putting it once more to her ear. She dialed 911 like her parents had taught her to do if there was ever an emergency and no one else was able to get help. Nope. There were no beeps when she pressed any of the numbers. There was no ringing that emanated through the little holes of the earpiece. No reassuring adult voice answered to offer her help and salvation.

An even heavier wave of hopelessness sought to crush Wren, weighing her down, wishing to smother her and grind her into the ground until she was nothing but a sad stain on the floor.

With a choked groan, she replaced the phone in its cradle and moved over to the couch. She climbed onto the middle cushion, the springs squeaking beneath, and leaned back, staring at the images moving around on the television screen. Some chef with a mustache and a huge hat was demonstrating kitchen knives. His knife cut easily through a tomato, making thin slices. He then moved on to a tin can, and finally a block of frozen spinach.

Wren grabbed the TV remote before pulling the afghan off the back of the couch and wrapping it around herself in its soft embrace. The fact that her hands and clothes were covered in paint-goo that would get all over the cushions and the blanket didn't matter. She would get in trouble for sure, but not as much as if she went outside by herself. Plus, she needed comfort. Her mother would understand. Maybe. Hopefully.

She would just sit here. Yeah. Sit and wait for someone to come home and help her. That's what Mom and Dad always told her to do whenever they went out somewhere crowded or unfamiliar.

If we ever get separated, you stay right where you are and we will come find you. Do not wander off. Do you understand?

That's what she intended to do then. Wren bundled herself in the blanket like a burrito, pointed the remote at the TV, changed the channel, and tried to focus her mind on whatever came up on the screen.

click

Another channel, another infomercial. A woman wearing

a multi-color leotard held a weird blue and red exercise device between her knees. As the woman squeezed her legs together, she claimed the device helped tone your thighs for that perfect figure. It looked dumb.

Wren changed to the next channel.

click

Now a man was trying to cover his bald spot with what looked like a can of spray paint. The paint covered the man's bald head but looked nothing like actual hair. Who would buy that stuff? If she had come across this commercial any night but tonight, Wren would've laughed her head off.

click

A woman with a lyrical accent, wearing a colorful scarf wrapped around her head, told the viewers to call her at the phone number appearing on the screen, and she would help with whatever problem they might need advice on. A sprig of hope briefly blossomed inside Wren's chest before being squashed when she had to remind herself that the phone wasn't working. She sighed, recalling that she wasn't supposed to talk to strangers anyway, even ones who appeared as friendly as this woman. Oh, how Wren wished she could contact this "Miss Cleo" and ask her what she should do.

Click

Her father appeared on the screen.

"Hey, Jellybean. You're up way past your bedtime."

9

THE RE-CORRECTION OF CHRIS

Jellybean.

Wren hated it whenever her dad called her by that nickname. But seeing him appear on the television screen, sitting in what looked like a plain white room, speaking directly to her, caused her heart to stutter for a beat. Her breath got caught in her lungs and her throat, holding on and not wanting to come out.

Her dad stared straight at her, his name appearing on a little blue banner underneath him as if he was being interviewed on the news: CHRISTOPHER ESPINOZA.

"Dad?" Wren's voice cracked as her throat constricted with a tight pain.

No, what was she doing? That's not how a TV worked. She couldn't talk to people on the screen. But why was her father on there? She must have accidentally switched over to the VCR and played some video tape he had made for whatever reason. He did that sometimes, making home movies of birthdays, anniversaries, and get-togethers. In fact, Grandma Manuela had suggested she and Wren get Dad a new camcorder for Father's Day this year.

Wren bit her bottom lip. She needed her actual right-now dad here, not a video-taped one.

"Dad, I need you," she sniffled, hoping the real Chris Espinoza would hear her and come swooping in. She wrapped the blanket even tighter around her shoulders. But if he was in the house, he would have come running at the sound of her screaming earlier. "Where are you?"

"I'm here," the image on the TV replied. "Don't you see me?"

He couldn't have been talking to her. Wren's eyes locked on the screen. The man on the television must have been speaking to someone off-camera.

"I'm here, Wren," TV-Dad said. He looked around himself at the empty white room he resided in. "I know you're probably really scared right now, but everything will be okay. I promise. I'm right where I'm supposed to be, doing what I need to do."

He is *talking to me.*

"Where are you really? I want you with me," Wren said, her hand holding a death grip on the remote control. "I need you here."

"I will be," her father answered. His face spread into a soft smile, the corners of his eyes crinkling. "We'll all be together soon enough."

"But upstairs, Grandma—"

"There's just something I need to do first," TV-Dad interrupted her. He glanced over to his right before scooting closer to the glass screen separating them. Now Wren could see her father's stubbly jaw in clearer detail, his unbrushed hair, the dark, heavy bags that hung under his eyes. "I've been unfair to you. So many times, I've put you in the middle of situations that you didn't need to be involved in. I've used you to create strain between me and your mother, even if I was doing it subconsciously. That was bad parenting on my part. I'm so sorry. And speaking of your mom, I've been unfair to her too. I haven't been taking into account her needs and respecting her work as much as I should have been. I've been a terrible husband to her."

Her dad had always been good to her and Mom. What he was saying wasn't true at all. She wondered if someone was forcing him to say these things.

"But we moved here because Mom wanted to!" Wren argued.

"I know, I know," TV-Dad said. He glanced off to the right again, his eyes lingering on something only he could see, before returning his gaze to Wren. "But it wasn't enough. Our fighting has affected you in ways we never wanted. Your mother is a truly wonderful person. I need to remember to submit more to what she wants, what she desires. It's not all about me. I've been so selfish lately. I need to always put her needs above my own. Above everything. I didn't understand that until we got to this house. Do *you* understand, Jellybean?"

Wren shook her head. Tears ran down her cheeks, leaving hot trail on her skin. None of this made any sense.

"No, I don't understand anything." she whispered.

Smiling, TV-Dad turned once more to look past the right edge of the screen.

"Dad, I need you," Wren croaked. She had to get her father to understand the desperate situation she was in. "There's this...this monster upstairs, and I don't know where Churro and Mom are. And Grandma...Grandma is...."

Before she could get all the words out, Wren noticed several dirty, red worms slither into frame, creeping along at a steady pace.

No, not worms.

Roots.

Those beet-red, root-like fingers she had seen upstairs

were now on the television, snaking their way over to her father. TV-Dad stared at them with a soft smile. They spread across the interior side of the screen in a manner that reminded Wren of a video she'd watched in school. The video had been of lots of different plants growing, only the footage was sped up so that it looked like everything grew at an incredible rate with disturbing, jerky movements.

"Dad, run!" The words burst by themselves out of her mouth.

Whether he was unable to hear her, or simply ignored her, she couldn't tell. TV-Dad stayed where he was in that blank, white room. The root fingers came to rest on his cheek. One of them traced the line of his unshaven jaw, caressing it. Then without warning, the roots wrapped themselves around his neck like a noose.

Without looking back at her, her father said, "You'll understand soon enough, Wren. Something wonderful is coming."

In a quick, violent motion, the roots tightened around his throat and yanked her dad out of frame. The blurry, split-second image of his body flying through the air looked almost cartoonish. The white room on the screen now sat empty.

Wren's entire body shook like she had swallowed a revving car engine. Her eyes could not look away from that white room, the image of her father and the roots burned into her retinas. Had that really been her father, though? What had happened to him?

That's when she heard it: a series of noises emanated from out of the television's speakers. Barely audible at first, the noises grew in volume until they filled the living room to the brim with the soundwaves. Wren couldn't begin to comprehend what she heard, except to say that whatever was happening, it sounded rough, sharp, abrasive.

And wet.

A swell of screaming soon joined the cacophony. It rose in pitch and intensity with every passing second, straining the capacity of the television's speakers until they crackled. Screaming, agonized screaming. Wren stared at that white room on the screen, listening to such unbelievable, ceaseless, throat-rending shrieking that she couldn't fathom how the owner of that butchered voice hadn't taken a breath yet. A chunk of something flew into frame and—

The video cut out and the screen turned to staticky snow.

The last echoes of that hideous screaming faded from inside her head, and Wren could do nothing but sit there on the sofa. One hand, she now realized held the remote control in a death grip, while her other hand held the blanket around herself so tightly that the fabric was cutting into her neck.

As she forced herself to relax, she became very aware of someone standing right behind the couch on which she sat. She had no idea how long her brain had been registering the presence, her attention having been enraptured with what was happening on the television. Now she could feel the hairs on the back of her neck standing on end, as if they were trying to detach themselves and escape, while an uncomfortable tingle crawled around on her scalp, and an intangible yet palpable pressure pushed against her shoulders.

"For her...."

The breathy words caused a few strands of hair on the back of her head to flutter in response. The voice was unknown to her ears, yet it possessed a familiar aspect to it.

Someone stood behind her, and Wren was filled with the sort of dread that made her feel hot and sick and terrified; a similar feeling as when she knew she was in trouble.

Turn around and look.

Don't look.

You have to look.

Don't look!

With a painful slowness, Wren's neck turned until she peered over her shoulder. Standing behind the couch was a figure that she could only describe as a "man-again"—one of those big, blank-faced dolls that stores used to display clothing. Except this one had no clothes on to display. And whereas the ones Wren had seen at the store had smooth, plastic skin, this "man-again" looked like its rubbery body had melted a bit all over. What was even weirder was—

The figure moved.

A dose of adrenaline shot through Wren's veins.

The figure leaned down over the back of the couch as if wanting a closer look at her. Wren attempted to leap away from it off the couch, but as she was still snugly burrito-wrapped in the blanket, her feet got tangled and her body went sprawling onto the floor, her head missing the coffee table by mere inches and her body barely cushioned as she landed on the thin area rug that Mom always said "brightened up the living room!"

The "man-again" continued to lean over the back of the couch with a stiff posture until it seemed to overbalance. It tumbled over, following Wren to the floor. She managed to scramble out of its way. But the figure was much taller than Wren, and did crash into the coffee table, breaking two of the table's legs and sending splinters of wood flying off into the shadowed recesses of the house. Wren felt a large chunk nick her left cheek, warm beads of blood trickling out.

The figure moaned in pain on the floor. Its cold, soft hand wrapped itself around Wren's ankle. In panicked instinct, she managed to kick it off while untangling her legs from the afghan, hurried to her feet, and made to bolt out of the room when the "man-again" spoke to her.

"Jellybean...."

Wren halted mid-step, stumbling before coming to a complete halt, frozen in horror.

"I'm...better now, Jellybean. It all...worked out. I'm so much better...than I ever thought...I could be."

The figure lying on the floor behind her continued to speak in a labored, wheezing voice. Why was it calling her that nickname, though? Wren knew why, but her mind wasn't trying to hide the answer from her. She just didn't want to accept it.

Her body and instincts fighting her the whole way, Wren turned around to look at the thing that had spoken to her.

In the flickering light of the TV screen, she got a better look at the figure now.

"...Dad?"

And it sickened her.

The "man-again" lay there on the floor, its head propped up at an awkward angle by the broken coffee table. Back at their old house, Wren had once found a beetle grub in the back yard. This person-thing sprawled on the floor reminded her of that gross bug she had poked at with a stick. Its lumpy white skin looked just like grub flesh: sickly pale and uncomfortably supple. But what disturbed Wren the most was the fact that if this was truly her father, then every identifying mark and physical trait she had ever known to make her dad who he was, was now somehow gone. Erased.

The figure moaning and squirming in front of her eyes was a blank, featureless man-shaped nothing. Its hairless, pliant grub-flesh now held no similarity to anything human, let alone anything resembling her father. The expressionless eyes, shapeless nose, and flabby lips betrayed nothing of the person she had seen moments ago on the TV; absolutely nothing of the man who had hugged her, fed her, and kissed her goodnight every day of her life.

Without her telling them to, Wren's legs backed her up several steps away from the pile of blobby amorphousness.

"Where...are you going, Jellybean?" her father—*it couldn't be, it just couldn't be*—croaked. The figure tried to sit up, but he appeared too weak to do more than wriggle on the ground like a helpless baby, unable to even lift its head. "Don't leave."

"What happened?" Wren whispered. Her stomach churned and roiled at the sight of her "man-again" dad, and she feared that if she spoke too loud or too long, she would throw up.

"I'm going to...to be good now," came the answer in a voice that resembled her dad's, even as it spilled out from those awful, flabby lips. "I've been made blank, new...fresh. Your mother...now she can rework me. I can be...whatever she wants me to be. What she needs me to be." It took a shuddering breath that rattled its entire gelatinous form. "I was dirty...tainted. No good for her. No good. Now I have been...wiped clean. It's all for the...better. Your mother will improve...me and she will improve you too. Don't you want to...be a masterpiece, Jellybean?"

Wren backed up farther as she shook her head. "No."

"Then you're an idiot!" her father yelled with such force that Wren flinched and stumbled backward. "Ignorant little fucking brat. I've been made pure! Can't you see that? My body will transcend this purity as well as all known beauty by the artistic touch of your mother's hand. You have no idea, Wren. No idea! Your mother will finally receive the recognition she deserves, and you won't stop her!"

The barrage of words were aimed at Wren's back, as she had already bolted from the living room. She couldn't stand the grotesque sight of her father-made-nothing, writhing back there on the ground, helpless and impotent. The yelling was worse, however. She had heard her dad yell before. Of course she had. Mom and Dad and fought and fought, their voices resounding throughout this house and the old one before it. Oh, they pretended as if Wren and Grandma Manuela couldn't hear them, but they heard.

Wren had heard, but never in her life had those hateful tones, that vicious anger, been aimed toward her. To hear her father spew such venom in her direction, mixed with the horror of seeing his new "reborn" form, expunged of everything that was him....

It was too much to handle. Too much for her young brain to process.

Too much.

Racing away down a short unlit hallway, Wren made for the front door. She didn't care that it was dark and raining outside. It didn't matter that she would be running out into the street on her own without parental supervision. Her mother would have to understand. This was an emergency. She needed to get help; help from anyone.

The front door was in sight.

Wren sped toward it, reaching out for the deadbolt, but instead of grasping it, her fingers hit a flat surface. Confusion and terror wrestled in the pit of Wren's belly as she again reached for the deadbolt, then for the doorknob. And again, her fingers were met with a flat, smooth surface.

She ran her palm in every direction over the door in front of her before flicking on the entryway light on the wall right next to her. As the light fixture came to life, Wren backed up to take in the entirety of the door.

Except it wasn't a door any longer.

Everything inside her seemed to squeeze into her throat.

It was a painting.

The front door of the house had been replaced with an exact replica made up of paints on a canvas. No giant frame encompassed it. Instead, the painting simply stood where a real door should've been. It was impossible. How could it be possible?

Wren pressed both palms against the painted door, moving them everywhere she could reach. She could feel no real door underneath the canvas, only a flat wall.

Desperate, Wren's fingers flew to the edge of the canvas, picking at it until they were able to worm themselves under. It took several tugs, but using all her might, fueled by urgency, despair, and terror, Wren managed to rip the bottom half of the painting away in a wide, ragged chunk with a loud tearing of fibers.

Her sense of touch had been right. Behind the canvas was only a solid wall.

A few sobs escaped Wren's mouth, and she hated how much like a baby she sounded in that moment. What was she to do, though? She had fallen asleep in a perfectly normal house in a perfectly normal world. Now she had woken up to more craziness and horror, more grotesqueness and unbelievability, than all the nightmares she'd ever had combined. Reality itself was breaking down. Or had it already shattered into a million irreparable pieces? Every time Wren believed she was putting reality back together, those jagged slivers would cut her hands. She couldn't do any of this on her own. She was only seven years old. But no one was here to help her. The people she relied upon for survival and guidance had been turned into surreal and hellish versions of themselves.

More sobs wiggled free from her throat followed by a flood of full-on bawling.

Wren fled from the front door to the laundry room. There was a door there that led to the garage. She could get out of the house that way. But as she burst into the laundry room, speeding past the washing machine and dryer, the nagging fear in the back of her mind slammed into her immediate consciousness.

The door to the garage was a painting as well.

"No!" she shrieked, before hurriedly retreating and making for the kitchen. The door to the backyard had to still be there. It just had to. Tripping over her own feet, bashing into furniture, Wren crashed through the house and into the kitchen. The back door sat right before her, its glass panes showing the night outside with its faintly glowing rain.

Her mind moving faster than she could process her own thoughts, Wren ran full tilt at the door. She wouldn't try the locks or the handles. She would jump and crash through the glass like she had seen so many people do in the action movies her dad and grandma loved to watch. She would burst through and once free from the house, continue running, never stopping until she reached help and safety.

Wren hit her top speed as she aimed for the pane of glass right in front of her.

"Let me go!" Her voiced rang out, bouncing off the kitchen walls to assault her own ears.

SMACK

The back door's glass didn't shatter or even crack. It absorbed all of Wren momentum and threw it back at her.

This door, too, was a painting.

Wren stood there dazed, bursts of light dancing before her eyes, snapping in and out of existence. A hot trickle of blood ran from her nose, but she felt no pain. Her entire nervous system was overloaded with boiling hysteria.

In a sudden frenzy, Wren pinballed around the kitchen, flinging open anything that she could lay her hands on. Cabinets, drawers, the refrigerator door—she threw them all wide open.

What was real and what was painted illusion? She had to check everything she could.

Everything.

Open the real. Have to open every door that's real!

The light from the yawning fridge, the pulsating darkness —everything spun around her in a swirling, throbbing vortex. In her manic whirlwind, Wren felt another knob fall into her hand and flung open the door it was attached to without hesitation. She did not know what door she had just opened or where it led, but she darted through it anyway, uncaring.

Slamming the door behind her, Wren collapsed into a fetal position on the ground, the spasms of her lung-tearing crying overwhelming her.

10

FIGURE WITH ROOTS

Wren had no idea how long she'd been shut in wherever she was. It seemed like hours had gone by while she lay there crying. Her meltdown before fleeing through the door had been a frightening moment. She had never experienced an outburst such as that. Utter hopelessness, smothering panic, and wild terror had roiled around inside her like a tornado. That explosive, raging storm of emotions had eased a little by now—eased, but not abated. The pot still simmered over the fire, ready to boil over the second the heat was turned up.

Getting up from the floor, Wren looked around at the complete blackness enveloping her, fully expecting some unseen hand to reach out and grab hold of her. When nothing happened, she felt for a switch in the direction she was sure she had come through. Her hands groped blindly in front of her before making contact with the door. Moving to the left, her fingers slid along the door, the wall, then, ah, the light switch. The bulb overhead came to life as she flicked on the switch, stabbing at her eyes as they had become accustomed to the veil of darkness. She found herself surrounded by shelves of glass jars, dried lentils, cereals, cans of soup, and packs of soda. A half-empty sack of rice sat slumped on the floor. She realized she had been cowering in the kitchen pantry.

What to do?

Wren knew she couldn't hide in the pantry forever. But did she really want to go back out into the house? The answer was most definitely "no." Would she have to courage to leave the pantry when the sun came up? Uncertainty ate away at her. She could simply wait until someone came to check on her and her family. Surely her school would eventually try to contact her parents to see why she wasn't in class. And the office would call her dad to see why he hadn't come into work.

Yes, she would eventually be discovered here if she just stayed put. There was plenty of food to eat to keep her alive for a good while. Well, she had no can opener, so those soups were out of the question. Still, there was...well, she couldn't cook the rice or the any of the other dried goods without a stove or something. The soda she could drink, and the cereal she could eat dry.

Cereal's on the top shelf, she thought as she looked upward. Would the shelving support her so that she could climb it? Falling down and crashing to the floor wasn't an appealing prospect.

And where would she go to the bathroom?

No, she couldn't just stay in here. There had to be a way out of the house. Not every exit could be a painting. Then again, she knew she couldn't apply any rational logic to this illogical situation. This was a nightmare come to life, and dreams operated on rules beyond comprehension. Wren could definitively say what would be possible or impossible in this situation.

A faint noise came from the other side of the door, out in

the kitchen. Wren hit the light switch on reflex, dousing the pantry once again in velvety darkness. She couldn't tell who or what was out there in the kitchen, and she didn't want the unknown entity to know where she was hiding.

Pressing her ear to the door, she strained her ears, listening. She tried to tune out the sound of the ceaseless patter of rain against the sides of the house, but as if sensing her intention, it grew louder, reverberating through the very bones of the structure, muffing all other noises.

She pressed her ear harder against the door.

Were those feet shuffling?

Maybe someone or some*thing* was moving around?

Then came the soft scrape of a chair's legs against the linoleum followed by a familiar creak.

Someone had sat down at the kitchen table.

A feeble glow in the corner of her vision caught Wren's attention, and she looked down toward her feet. Her bare toes were awash in a dim yellow light coming from under the door.

Could it be the sunrise?

It's morning!

If the sun was coming up, that meant the night was over. The sun brought daylight, and Wren knew that daylight vanquished the darkness and all the ghouls and boogeymen that came with it.

Relief flooded through her in a tidal wave of cleansing waters, washing away the terror that had polluted her sanity. If it was now morning, she no longer had to hide here in the pantry for days until somebody showed up looking for her. The thought of leaving the pantry and exposing herself to the lurking danger proved too debilitating when night blanketed the world. The promise of the sunlit day, however, doused her anxiety and worry. She now knew the answer to her previous concerns. Yes, the daytime returned the courage that the night stole away. She would not have to cower in the pantry for days on end.

"I'm here!" Wren exclaimed as she threw open the pantry door. She expected to see Grandma Manuela, fully restored to her normal self, sitting at the kitchen table, as she was always the first to get out of bed. Churro would be sitting at her side, as he was wont to do, patient yet eager as he waited for any bit of breakfast to fall to the floor.

But no. None of that was there.

Wren stepped out of the safety of the pantry and into the same night-drenched kitchen. The faint light that had reached under the pantry door, she now realized, came from the refrigerator which she had flung open during her manic frenzy. Wren felt weighed down, like an anchor had been thrown around her neck—not only from disappointment, but also from feeling stupid for not realizing where the light had been coming from.

Such a stupid idiot, she thought. Just like her fresh, blank father had said she was.

The fridge rumbled, struggling to maintain its set temperature as the open door released both its cold and its light. The sound drew Wren out of her self-pitying thoughts. Turning toward the kitchen counter, she looked at the green numbers that glowed on the microwave's display to see just how far off the sun might be from coming up.

2:50am, the large blocky numbers informed her.

No. That...made no sense. Unless she had somehow severely misread the clock on her nightstand, it was still the exact same time it had been when she'd gotten up to pee.

She clenched her eyes closed for a moment before opening them to look once again at the microwave clock, then over at the oven's red digital readout. The both said the same thing.

2:50am.

Closing her eyes once more, Wren forced down her rising panic. Inside her head she counted out sixty seconds, then decided to continue to one hundred and twenty. That would mean at least two minutes had passed.

When she opened her eyes and looked again, neither clock had changed.

No, no, no. What did this mean? Her heart sinking in despair, Wren wished she could somehow pluck one of the smiley-faced suns off of her pajamas and throw it into the sky to brighten the world and end this awful night.

"So pretty."

Wren started, almost tripping backward at the unexpected voice, although a fleeting, self-recriminating thought told she should expect such unexpected things by now. This house—or at least something within it that was *not* part of her family—was playing with her the way a cat toyed with its tiny, defenseless victim.

The light from the still-open fridge spilled out in a narrow column that ran over the kitchen table, dividing it in half. Wren squinted at the shadowed half of the table and then recoiled when she could make out a more solid chunk of darkness that sat there. Its precise shape and size were impossible to discern without more light, but conflicting emotions made Wren uncertain whether or not she really wanted to see the presence clearly.

"So pretty," it repeated in a voice Wren had heard before. A thick, wet voice that sounded as if it were speaking through a mouthful of syrup.

A creaking, scraping sound reached Wren's ears just as she saw long, gnarled roots, ten of them, slither out of the dark, across the plastic checkered tablecloth and onto the illuminated half of the table. They stopped when they reached the end, curling around the edge and gripping it with such force that the wood of the table groaned and cracked.

As Wren stood only a few feet away, she could see every bump, knot, and thin offshoot of the beet-red root fingers where they lay in the column of light.

It took her several attempts to swallow the massive, dry cork that had formed in her throat, blocking her airway. When her throat cleared, Wren said the first thing that came to mind.

"Who...Who are you?"

Whatever it was that those root fingers belonged to didn't reply to her question, and despite her heart telling her not to look, she found her curiosity compelling her to strain her eyes in an effort to make out more details of the entity still cloaked in shadow. Where Wren guessed its head might be— assuming the thing had a human-like anatomy—a disordered collection of spots appeared and reflected the refrigerator light. The red fingers flexed and squeezed the table's edge.

It took every ounce of courage inside her for Wren to ask again:

"Who are you?"

"You must imagine me so I can be," came the flat, unemotional response.

What did that even mean? Adults often talked about many things that Wren didn't understand. So maybe that explained her inability to grasp the meaning of what this thing was trying to convey to her with those enigmatic words. She didn't know why—it was like some instinctive knowledge deep down inside the innermost part of her brain had bubbled to the surface—but Wren suspected this entity wasn't just the age of an adult, but older. Much, much older. A primordial fear, something she had never felt before, squeezed her heart.

"I don't get what you mean," she managed to say. She kept grabbing at her own hands to keep them from trembling.

"Lower minds can never comprehend higher motives."

That thick, viscous voice made Wren's skin crawl. Her brain felt dirty and greasy just hearing it and letting its words bounce around in her skull. Still, she had no clue as to what the shadow at the kitchen table was trying to get at.

"Who..." she began again, then swallowed. "*What* are you?"

The fingers flexed again. The wood of the table sounded like it was about to splinter. The sound of a heavy inhalation and then exhalation emanated from the shadowed form at the table, and the entire house seemed to take a breath along with it. That multitude of dots--that reflected the fridge light flickered in the darkness. Despite the fact that she couldn't see its face—or even be sure it possessed a face in the same manner a human did—Wren could tell the presence was smiling at her.

"Imagine me so I can be. An idea takes root," the red fingers flexed, "it must be expressed in the most ideal manner. Cultivated and nurtured. I guide the brush. I guide the charcoal, the chisel. Through the expression of the tool, I manifest. My gateway into actuality."

Wren's mind took these statements in, trying to make what her dad would call "heads or tails" of their meanings.

"So, people need to imagine you? So, like, we created you?"

"Little bitch!" the entity roared, shaking the whole house. Even the sound of the ceaseless rain froze for several seconds before resuming its deluge in a loud, hard smacking against the roof and walls. The root fingers curled into two fists and pounded angrily on the table.

Wren swore she heard the table crack from the impact, and she shrank away from the vocalized fury. Again, without seeing, only knowing, Wren was certain that invisible smile had turned into an unseen snarl of disgust at her words.

"I am no *creation*." It said the word with utter disdain. "I am inspirator, inciter, enkindler. I am muse."

Frustration joined fear inside her as most of those words had no meaning for Wren. They were beyond any vocabulary she had learned thus far in school. "Muse" was familiar, though, from TV and through books. And of course she had heard her mother use it every now and then in regards to her artwork. Wren understood it to mean what inspired an artist. But she had never been really sure if the word referred to a person or an idea or something else entirely too abstract for her to recognize.

This thing was calling itself a muse. A muse to who? Was it—

"Your mother," it said, as if finishing the thought for her. The fury in its voice had subsided, replaced with an air of arrogance. "She is gifted. More so even than Isidoro Cervantes. Oh, he came close, but in the end he failed. Your mother...talented, obsessed, self-absorbed...is perfect for me."

"Where is my mom?" Wren asked. Running the back of her hand over her face, she realized she had broken out into a distraught sweat despite the cold that cut down to her bones.

"You know already," came the answer, a hint of amusement suffusing the words.

A door right outside the kitchen opened on creaking hinges. Wren didn't need to turn her head to know which door had just opened. The shiver that ran through her body rattled her so much it made her nauseous. Of course she knew where her mother was; the place she always was.

"Go, pretty pretty. Go down and see."

Not looking away from where the presence sat at the dark end of the table, not even allowing herself to blink,

Wren made her way out of the kitchen, walking backward. When she could no longer see the kitchen table, she turned toward the door that had apparently opened by itself.

Her mother was down there. Any other time, Wren would assume her mom would be working on her paintings down in the basement-turned-studio.

But who knows what's happening to Mom right now? she thought. She shook her head before terrifying scenarios could manifest themselves inside her mind.

"Mom?" Wren called into the basement after a moment's hesitation. She could see that there were lights on down below. The wooden, doglegged stairs—which looked much longer and steeper than she had ever remembered them being—were dimly lit where they turned the corner.

"Come on down, sweetie," her mother's voice floated up the stairs, beseeching in a sugary tone that she never used.

Still, Wren couldn't resist, and stepped over the threshold and down onto the first step. Part of her expected the basement door to slam shut behind her. Instead, it closed with infinite slowness, as if taunting her to make a run for it while she could. Gathering her courage, she remained where she stood as it clicked shut.

She knew it would've been pointless to do anything but descend. Plus, she had to see her mom, and perhaps help her however she could.

You weren't able to help Dad or Grandma Manuela.

Shut up!

You know it's true.

She tried to push the thoughts away, but they insisted on lingering.

One hand trailing along the wall, as much for balance as for the small sense of security it offered, Wren took her time going downward, putting both feet on each step before readying herself for the next one. Every time the stairs creaked and groaned under her, Wren cringed and had to fight the urge to rebuke them with a shush. Her mother already knew she was coming down the staircase, yet Wren still felt like she should be as silent and inconspicuous as possible.

Step.

Step.

Pause.

After what had happened with Dad and Grandma Manuela, Wren did not want to see what awaited her at the bottom of the stairs. What horrifying state would her mother be in?

Step.

Step.

Pause.

How did she know that had even been her mother who had answered her? That presence with the root fingers...what was it? Had the monstrous forms of her father and grandma really been her family members? Or had this entity created them?

How could she know anymore what was real in this nightmare house?

Step.

Step.

Pause.

11

THE PAINTER AND THE PUPPET

Why were there so many more stairs than what Wren remembered?

Whatever the reason was for this warping of reality, she had to see what had become of her mother. Whether these encounters were really with her family members or grotesque creations of the dark presence didn't matter. Wren was determined to find a way to help them. She had to, or she would lose everything.

"Why are you taking so long coming down?" her mom called from around the corner. "Stop dilly-dallying already, I want to show you something."

With a deep breath to calm her nerves and steel her resolve, Wren rushed down the rest of that too-long staircase, finally speeding around the corner and leaping over the last two steps to land with a thud on the concrete floor at the bottom.

The basement that was also her mother's art studio—occupied by paint splattered tables laden with art supplies, cans of acetone, easels, and dirty rags—was lit by several spotlights and floor lamps, highlighting the plethora of paintings; most of them hung up on the walls, but some scattered about the floor in haphazard stacks, or tucked away in dusty corners, leaning on one another. Many of these paintings were her mom's own artwork, but Wren recognized the majority as those of Isidoro Cervantes. There were depictions of mutilated people, nauseating human-animal hybrids, corrupted landscapes, and buildings of illogical design that radiated menace. Wren had never seen subjects such as these in the paintings her mom had shown before. The ones displayed upstairs were creepy and haunting for sure. But these were hellish and grotesque. There was no doubt, however, that the style was Isidoro's.

Her mother had been busy. Very busy. She hadn't been creating her own artwork for quite some time it seemed, but had been fervently restoring all of Isidoro's paintings back to their former glory. The old works of art, if they could be called that, were now as pristine as the day Isidoro Cervantes had painted them.

"There you are," her mother said. An excited giggle followed.

The Isidoro Cervantes paintings, along with the strong smell of paint and chemicals that stung her nose, made Wren feel woozy, and it took it a moment to locate from where exactly her mom's voice had emanated from. At the back of the basement, next to a corner piled with dusty, unfamiliar furniture, was a curtained-off area. Lights behind the white curtain outlined the clear silhouette of her mother standing before what looked like a tall easel. This featureless shadow looked to be painting with large, sweeping strokes, followed by exaggerated flourishes with the brush.

"Mommy." The word rasped in Wren's throat. She hadn't called her mother by that name since last year, when she decided that she was too old to address her parents as "Mommy" and "Daddy."

"I'm so glad you're here, Wren!" The outline of her mother set down the brush on the easel and took a step back to admire her own work. There was an odd, disjointed quality in the silhouette's movements that disturbed Wren.

"We need to leave and get help," Wren said. She realized then that she was shivering from head to foot. "Something bad happened to Dad and Grandma."

"I'm so excited, Wren," the silhouette of her mom continued, ignoring Wren's statements. "You have no idea how excited. I've been working so hard on restoring the Cervantes paintings. He was a genius. None of his peers could ever compare to him. It's a shame no one ever saw that when he was alive. It makes me not just sad, but angry. An absolute genius.... But sometimes genius does lead to craziness. I guess your father was right about one thing at least. Cervantes did vandalize his own paintings. It's still hard to believe that an artist of such caliber would do such a thing to the incredible artwork he poured his soul into."

There was a pause as her mother's silhouette froze, then slumped over as if she had somehow fainted while remaining on her feet.

"Mom?" Wren's voice shook. "Are you okay?"

A silence stretched on for several minutes. The urge to flee back upstairs and the urge to run over and rip the curtain aside pulled Wren in different directions. But before she could make a decision, the silhouette popped back up, the outline of its arm flailing about with the paintbrush in its hand.

"Now, I know what you're thinking, Wren," her mom went on, as if nothing had happened. "How could I differentiate between Isidoro's artwork and the paint he splattered on the canvas? I just knew. Something inside me, whispering to me. It guided my hand. I'm so glad we moved into this house." A satisfactory moan. "What I couldn't predict was what I would find under all that paint Isidoro poured over the paintings. But I worked so hard. I restored and uncovered so much. And now I finally did it, Wren. This last painting...I uncovered Isidoro Cervantes' masterpiece."

From behind the curtain, her mother lifted a hand to point. No, that wasn't right. It looked to Wren like her mom's hand *was lifted,* as if a string was tied around her wrist and yanked upward by something unseen.

Apprehensive about taking her eyes off the silhouette of her mom for even an instant, Wren forced her eyes to follow her mother's finger to where it indicated a canvas lying on a central table. She crept over, trying to make as little noise as possible, although she wasn't sure why, since her mother already knew she was there.

What else might be listening? she wondered.

The table was taller than the others, at about Wren's eye level. Wiping her sweaty palms on her pajama pants, she reached up to grasp the edges of the unframed canvas, and pulled it down. Her gut clenched tight as she anticipated what Isidoro Cervantes' "masterpiece" might depict.

It was a canvas, painted black.

And nothing more.

There seemed to be no visible brush strokes or any variation in the tone of the color. The entire canvas was just a void of unrelenting blackness.

"There's nothing on it," she said in a small voice, afraid that her mother might get angry at her inability to discern the greatness and meaning in the art.

The clinking of metal rings warned Wren that her mom had pulled aside the curtain she had been painting behind. The slap of bare feet and the quick cessation told her that her mother now stood right behind her. The pungent odor—Wren's mind could only compare it to spoiled meat and blackening fruit—that she now caught an unfortunate whiff of as it wafted over her, left no doubt that something was most definitely wrong here.

"Well, there's nothing on it at the *moment*," her mother said from behind. "He was under all that paint for so long, he wanted some time to get out and breathe."

At those words, as in incomprehensible as they were, Wren felt overrun with a sense of imminent danger. She whirled around to demand that they leave the house this instant.

But as soon as her eyes fell upon her mom, Wren's mind stuttered, and she forgot the words she was going to say.

Her mother stood there before her, hair in a messy bun and wearing the pajama shorts and tank top, now stained with splotches of dark paint, she usually wore to bed. That was where normality ended.

Her mother looked down at Wren with a loving smile; the kind of smile she had once worn when she would wake Wren up in the mornings or pick her up from school. This smile, however, was etched into skin that had turned a mottled, grayish-greenish hue; the color of mold. Her mother's entire body looked not just diseased, but already dead.

Wren recoiled in revulsion at the sight.

The worst part, though....

The worst part....

Wren's brain tried to make sense of how it was possible to see what she was seeing. How was her mother walking, talking, painting?

Every joint, every major point of articulation on her mother's body had been severed. Neck, knees, wrists, waist, elbows, hips, all the rest—each one of them had been cut through and detached. Instead of the normal joints and connective tissues, what held the segments of her mom together, protruding from each site of separation, were thick, gnarled, beet-red roots.

Awe-struck, enthralled, stupefied, Wren let the canvas fall from her hands. Invisible spikes had been driven into her feet, for she could not move them. In fact, no muscle in her entire body want to work properly.

"What's wrong?" her mother asked through that unsettling smile that still dominated her horrifying visage. It was then, looking up at that familiar yet haunting face, that Wren realized her mom's eyes had been sewn shut with tiny roots. "Don't you want to see what I've been working on?"

Again, her mom's arm jerked upward like a marionette's limb on a string, and waved a limp hand toward the open curtain she had only recently been painting behind. Wren turned her head slowly in the indicated direction. On a large easel sat a misshapen canvas. It was not square or rectangular as a painting should be, but instead it was shaped like an irregular blog with ragged, uneven edges. Upon it a door had been painted. It appeared to be their front door, though Wren noticed it was incomplete. The doorknob was missing, not having been painted in yet.

While trying to process what possible meaning this painting could contain and why her mother was so intent on showing it to her, Wren realized there was something off about that canvas her mother had used. A lot of the canvas's white base color was still visible patches. The material possessed weird bumps and ridges; a strange, indefinable texture. Next to the easel, on top of a stool, sat a bowl of paint. A bowl that looked jagged and dirty with long gray hairs still attached to it, sprouting from it.

Understanding hit Wren like a punch to the chest.

"Dad....Grandma...." she whispered, horrified.

"Don't worry about them," her mother purred. "They've become so much more now. Transcendence, Wren. Do you know what that word means? They are so much more now.

People are fleeting, but art last forever, able to be admired for generations to come."

Reaching into her shorts pocket, Wren's mom pulled out a yellow utility knife. Thumb on the slider, she pushed out the blade from its casing.

click, click, click

Wren gulped so forcefully her ears popped.

"Art is the purest form of expression," her mother said. She raised her free hand up to her face, inspecting it. "It is immortal. It makes the artist immortal as well. We can live forever."

With a swift motion, Wren's mother brought the extended blade across the tips of her rotten fingers. The knife cut through them like they were made of nothing more than Play-Doh. The fingertips toppled to the floor with a soft patter.

"Don't you want to live forever with me, Wren?"

She brought her mutilated fingers to Wren's face, the stumps oozing blood so dark it was black. Whimpering, Wren stood petrified to the spot as her mother proceeded to smear her bloody fingers all over Wren's face, tracing shapes and symbols. Some of it dripped down into her nostrils. The foul smell made her stomach churn.

"Be with us, Wren." Her mother pulled her hands away from Wren's face. Wriggling and writhing out of the severed finger stumps, red roots began to emerge like worms. "Be with us forever, and we will make the prettiest art."

Before she could even fully take in everything that was happening, an explosion of barking and thumping on the basement door above snapped Wren out of her miring thoughts.

"Churro? Churro!"

That was it, she was done. Wren knew she had to get out of the house immediately. It didn't matter if all the doors and windows had been replaced with paintings, she would escape, even if that meant taking a spoon and digging through a wall to the outside. She needed help. The police, the fire department, the army; she needed help.

Wren regained control of her legs just as her smiling, fragmented mother reached out to grab her in an ungainly, disjointed movement. Cold fingers and roots brushed the back of her neck as Wren turned and bolted for the stairs. On her hands and feet like an animal, she scrambled up the staircase, now back to normal length, toward the basement door, screaming her throat raw. Churro's whining and barking grew louder with each step as she clambered up, closer and closer to the door. She just had to pray it wasn't locked.

Wren rounded the corner of the dogleg and the top of the staircase came into view. As she reached the landing, Wren gathered all the strength she could muster and leapt upward. She grabbed the doorknob and twisted it so hard, she feared it would come off in her little hands.

Nonetheless, the door opened and she rocketed through, slamming it closed behind her.

And found herself *not* in the kitchen.

THE GREAT DAY OF HIS MASTERPIECE

A long, narrow corridor stretched out before Wren. Its highly polished black marbled floor separated two walls colored a deep crimson. Ornate crystal chandeliers hung from the high, arched ceiling at regular intervals, alternating with sconces that were placed along the walls, each holding a pair of candles. The lighting was simultaneously dim, yet offered a perfect amount of light to view the hallway's contents. For between the scones on both sides of the hallway were what had to be picture frames. From where she stood, her back pressed against (what had been) the basement door in (what used to be) their new, normal house, Wren could see giant rectangles lined the walls in between the scones. Each rectangle had been draped with a red velvet curtain, obscuring what she was sure were picture frames underneath so that she that she couldn't their contents.

Did she even want to know what lay hidden from view? She hoped they weren't more Isidoro Cervantes paintings.

"Dad, Grandma, Mom." She sniffled then looked around. "Churro?"

Her dog wasn't here, not that she could see, and there didn't seem to be anywhere here that he could hide. The corridor ended at a wall about fifty yards ahead where she could make out another frame, facing her, though a sheet had been draped over it as well.

With nowhere to go but forward, Wren took a tentative step, expecting some booby trap to go off or for her foot to sink into the reflective marble flooring as if it were the surface of a pond. When her toes pressed against solid ground, she put her full weight down and skulked down the corridor, hoping there was some exit she just couldn't see from where she stood.

As she stepped down the corridor, she passed the first pair of covered frames on either side of her.

fwoosh

The red curtains obscuring the frames dropped to the ground of their own accord, revealing what lay underneath. On either side of her, ornate frames of black wood enclosed paintings of life-size adult human skeletons wrapped in constricting red roots that wound around their bones like snakes squeezing their prey.

Wren wanted to bolt, but noticed bronze plaques beneath both paintings. Perhaps whatever they said could be of some help in saving her family. Taking a deep breath, she approached the painting on the right. She shivered. Those bones were so life-like.

With disappointment, Wren saw that the bronze plaque was engraved with what she assumed was a name and nothing else. She read the name, pronouncing it in her head.

SOBEKHOTEP

Wren wondered if it really was a name, since she had never heard of such a person, although the sound of it reminded her of something out of one of her books on ancient Egypt.

Turning, she gazed at the other uncovered painting. The tightly bound skeleton in this one had it jaw wrenched open by the enveloping roots, and looked as if the individual had died screaming. The name on this painting's plaque was a bit difficult for Wren to figure out the pronunciation.

HIERONYMUS BOSCH

"Hee-er-on-nee...muss?"

No, enough of this. She was getting distracted. She had to get out of here.

"Want to see the rest of my collection, pretty pretty?" The thick, heavy voice came from nowhere and everywhere.

Without pausing to consider, Wren put her legs into gear and raced down the corridor. Her entire body was exhausted after everything she had gone through tonight, but she forced herself to keep going. She had to get out.

As she flew past each single frame in the corridor, their sheets were pulled off by an invisible force. Each depicted in nightmarish detail a skeleton bound in those beet-red roots. It was a color she never ever wanted to see again for the rest of her life.

Pumping her legs as fast as they would go, and swinging her head from side to side, Wren managed to catch glimpses of more of the plaques as their sheets were yanked off.

fwoosh

PIETER BRUEGEL

SALVATOR ROSA

fwoosh

ODILON REDON

TSUKIOKA YOSHITOSHI

fwoosh

CARAVAGGIO

FRANZ VON STUCK

Dozens of paintings. Dozens of names.

For some unfathomable reason, these names seared

themselves into her mind. She recognized some of them, though from where, she couldn't remember at the moment. The corridor seemed to lengthen as she ran. New archways leading to other corridors appeared to open up in the walls at random intervals. Corridors with more frames filled with more skeletons. All appointed with plaques no doubt engraved with the names of those collected by the entity with the root fingers. She couldn't try to read them all.

So many people.

Finally, Wren reached the end of the hallway and the last of the paintings. The solitary frame that had faced her when she first entered the corridor still maintained its covering, but the two frames on either side had had their concealing veils ripped away as she reached them, just like the rest of the paintings that lined the walls. She stood transfixed.

The portrait to her left portrayed her mother, wrapped in those infernal roots like the other paintings. But unlike the others, this was not a skeletonized version of her mother, nor was it the disjointed, segmented mother from the basement. This was her mother as she had always been: full of life and normal.

Just then, the painting of her mother moved. The photorealistic representation of her mom, created by expert brushstrokes and skilled coloring, was inside that life-size portrait, now writhing and struggling against the roots that gripped her.

The painting's eyes met Wren's, and she knew without any doubt that this was her true mom.

"Wren, sweetie," the painted lips said, the words strained but calm. "You have to get out of here. Get out of the house. Don't let it get to you, please."

"Mommy."

"Just get out," she ordered. "Get out of here and away

from this damn house." Her painted arms fought with the roots tightening around them.

"I-I can go get help," Wren said. She could feel her heartbeat in every part of her body, her pulse ever quickening.

"No." Her mom stopped struggling and shook her head. "It's never going to let me go. It never lets anyone go.

She nodded at the portrait across the corridor facing her. Wren turned to look. Another trapped skeleton, the plaque on this one reading ISIDORO CERVANTES.

"Here, in my pocket," her mother said, catching Wren's attention again and indicating her shorts. "Hurry, get it."

Hesitating only briefly, Wren reached up, paused for another second, then reached her hand into the painting. If she hadn't already been through everything she had this night, she would've been amazed or perhaps convinced she was dreaming. Her hand had actually gone inside the painting as if it were an open window, and nothing more. The only sensation was that of minor resistance, like her hand was moving through a substance much thinner than water.

She had to stand on her tiptoes to reach inside the pocket of her mom's shorts. Felt an object with her fingertips and stretched farther to grasp it. When she had it clasped between her middle and index fingers, she pulled it out of the painting.

It was a paintbrush with a glob of white paint on its bristles.

"Hurry, go," her mother urged, jutting her chin to indicate the painting to Wren's right, the only one still covered by a sheet

With a nod, Wren walked over to the last frame to stand before it. The curtain moved with the slightest billow.

"Hurry, Wren."

Wren grabbed a fistful of the red curtain and ripped it down, unveiling the final painting. Before her was no depiction of a skeleton, but rather the unfinished likeness of the house's front door. It was the same painting her nightmare-mother had been working on in the basement. Wren's blood froze as she remembered what the canvas and paint were made out of.

Her stomach churned, but she held it back.

"Finish it and get out of here, sweetie," her mother instructed from her ornately-framed prison, her deep sorrow and regret evident in her voice. "I'm sorry. I did this to us. It's all my fault. My stupid obsessions." She began crying. Wren had never seen her mother cry before, and the sight hurt her in a way she didn't fully comprehend. "You have to get out. I don't want it to get you too."

"But you have to come too!"

"Just go!"

Brush in hand, Wren faced the painting of the door. She understood right away what she needed to do. Using the paint already on the brush, Wren drew a circle where the door's knob should be, then filled it in as best she could. It looked much cruder than the rest of the painting, but it would have to do.

Just as she'd done moments ago, Wren took a deep, steadying breath and then reached into the canvas. Again, there was that sensation of minor resistance. Her hand grasped the doorknob. Despite the gooey, tackiness of the fresh paint, the knob felt mostly solid and real in her hand.

She twisted it and the door opened with a tearing, sucking sound.

Once the door was fully open, she darted into the painting and over the threshold—

"Go, Wren. Get out of here!"

—onto the front porch of their house.

All was calm, silent. The rain had finally stopped. The lawn glistened with beads of water, and the asphalt just beyond the gate reflected the moonlight in the shallow pools it had collected.

For the first time that night, joy filled Wren like an overflowing cup. She jumped into the air and let out an actual whoop.

"Mom!" She ran back toward the door. Maybe if she could get her mom's portrait out of the house, she could find some adults who would know how to save her. "There's a way out!"

But the open front door, she now saw, only led back into the house as it always had. Gone were the long, terrifying corridors lined with paintings of skeletons. The momentary hope that had blossomed inside her chest wilted. Was there still a chance to get back to that nightmarish gallery and save her mom? What about Dad and Grandma Manuela? And she still hadn't seen any sign of Churro, she realized.

Stop lollygagging! You're out! Go get help already! Wren chastised herself.

Right, she needed to find some adults. Adults could handle this. Lots of adults.

Hopping off the porch, Wren hurried down the rain-soaked walkway until she reached the iron pedestrian gate in the fence that separated their yard from the street.

She grabbed the latch, eager to slide it back.

It dissolved in her hand, thick, black ooze running between her fingers and down her arm.

"Huh?" Even with everything she had been through, Wren couldn't suppress her shock.

"Silly, naïve child," came a familiar, thick voice.

All around her, before her very eyes, the neighborhood began to lose structure and melt. The gate, the trees, the houses, the cars, the moon, even the sky. Waterfalls of color splashed down as the world deliquesced. Reality itself was liquefying, and all Wren could do was stand there in utter disbelief and horror as she was splattered in paint from all directions.

"You're not going anywhere, pretty pretty." That syrupy voice bore directly into Wren's head.

Up above in the dissolving sky, a cluster of stars appeared.

They blinked.

No, not stars.

Wren screamed as roots started to grow out of the heaps and puddles that had been her world.

"Stop screaming, the door is open. Now, Wren, let's make something beautiful."

EPILOGUE

VANITAS STILL LIFE GOES ON

The museum curator took the glasses from his nose, wiped them with a handkerchief from his suit jacket pocket, then replaced them. He stared at the paintings arrayed before him, so enraptured by what he saw that he regretted his need to blink.

Finally, he turned to the woman who stood next to him, her arms held behind her back.

"I've got to say, Mrs. Espinoza, this is incredible." It was more than incredible, but the curator's reeling mind couldn't find the words sufficient to describe what had been brought to him. "Almost all of the Cervantes works are either in Spain or in Los Angeles. I was lucky enough a few years ago to acquire just one to display here in the museum. But this...."

Words now failed him completely, and he had to urge his brain to function as it should, though he couldn't fault its malfunction. It was an appropriate response.

Rebecca Espinoza smiled at him, waiting for him to continue.

When he was finally able to convey his thoughts, the

curator said, "They never found any new works in the house when Cervantes's son sold it. At least, that's what those who inquired were told. I *knew* he had to have painted something while he was locked up there. But for him to have created this amount of work?" He waved a hand to indicate the canvases. "This is quite extraordinary."

"They were well hidden in the house," she said, "I can assure you. It was a miracle that I found where he had hidden them all. It was like something guided me to them."

The curator nodded. "Yes, something must have."

A part of him wished the woman would go away. He just wanted to take all these paintings into his office and look them over in solitude, with nothing else to distract him. A deep yearning had ignited inside of his core—a fire that was stoked, fiercer and fiercer, each time his gaze fell upon them. It begged him to study the art, to pore over every minute detail of those desolate, macabre landscapes, and haunting, grotesque figures that had been so expertly rendered upon these canvases by the hand of a virtuoso.

"Isidoro Cervantes was truly a god among artists," the curator breathed out.

Rebecca made an odd, nasally sound before replying. "He really was. It's awful that such a genius mind was taken so soon when he should have had so much more time in this world to create. But with his Muse gone, life might have seemed pointless. Sad, but true for many."

"Yes, Luciana leaving him must have been the biggest of blows."

Rebecca began saying something else, but the curator paid her no attention.

"Such a treasured find," he interrupted, and ran a gloved finger over the edge of one of the paintings. This particular masterpiece had caught his attention when he first reviewed the astonishing collection of artwork Rebecca Espinoza had brought in. The piece depicted a world that appeared to be in the midst of warping and melting. Trees, houses, fences, telephone poles, even the moon and sky, all still retained enough of their shapes for the viewer to recognize them for what they were, yet each had been distorted to an uncomfortable degree, as if the reality in which this scene took place had lost all of its substance in an instant. And at the very center of the canvas was a child—a young girl no older than seven or eight years. While the unsettling and eldritch quality of the scene was typical of Cervantes in the latter half of his career, the subject itself, while painted in the usual stark shadows and rich, dramatic colors, was not one of Cervantes's usual ghoulish characters, and was at contrast with the rest of the disturbing world that entrapped her. The girl's legs were frozen in mid-run, while her arms had been thrown up as if to defend herself from curious red roots that snaked after her. The expression on her face was one of pure terror. Each of these elements was undeniably Cervantes.

The creation as a whole was so unusual. But there was Isidoro Cervantes's signature, right at the bottom.

"This piece, you're positive it was with the rest of these paintings?"

"Yes," Rebecca replied. "I found them all together. Why?"

"There's just something about this one." The curator chewed on the inside of his cheek for a moment. "I can definitely see Cervantes's style in it. It's obvious. But it also appears like someone else had a hand in it as well."

"Maybe Cervantes was trying something new with this one?" Rebecca offered.

The curator looked into the woman's eyes, but averted his gaze before too long. He could have sworn, for the briefest of seconds, that Rebecca Espinoza's eyes had flashed, like a cat's eyes reflecting light in the dark. "Yes, maybe," he muttered.

Looking back at the odd painting, the curator did a

double-take. The girl staring out of that canvas now had a thin streak of red running down her left cheek, almost as if she had cried it. That hadn't been there before, had it? The curator didn't think so. Studying the artwork as he had been, he would have remembered such a vital detail. The compulsion to touch that red line overcame him, and he pressed a light finger to the girl's face.

The red paint came away, staining the glove he wore. He had wiped away the child's bloody tear somehow.

"Everything okay?" Rebecca asked.

"Yes," the curator answered immediately. He felt like he should keep what had just happened to himself, though he wasn't sure why. Hiding his hand, he looked for an appropriate subject change to divert attention. "You know, I am reminded of Cervantes's famous 'Paintbrush of Immortality' quote. Do you know it?"

Mrs. Espinoza laughed. "Isidoro Cervantes is my biggest inspiration. Of course I know the quote. By heart, I may add." She cleared her throat, with a thick, distasteful sound. "It goes, 'A few strands of horsehair attached to a stick. The potential contained within such a small and humble instrument as the paintbrush is immeasurable. Unfathomable. With a dab of paint, a single stroke can herald the coming of a masterpiece. The coming of immortality. The oldest fear suffered by mankind is that of death. And for as long as that fear has persisted, so too has the hope of overcoming it. We have not achieved the means to live forever, and I do not believe we will. At least, not in my lifetime. But the artist does achieve immortality. Of a sort. If he is able to create that perfect kind of art, the kind that gains notice, that turns heads, that evokes in others true emotion, then that artist has created a legacy of his very own that will endure for generation upon generation, until all who are able to marvel at such glory cease to exist….And it is all possible because of the simple paintbrush.'"

The curator nodded. "I'm impressed you know the entire thing. That quote always gives me goosebumps. In a good way, of course." He chuckled, but quickly composed himself. "Well, I can tell you right now, the museum will pay you well for all these paintings. They would be a tremendous addition to our collection."

That close-lipped smile—*hiding teeth*, the curator thought for some reason he couldn't place, *hiding something worse*—remained plastered on Rebecca's face. "I don't want to sell them to you."

"Oh?" The curator tried to keep his voice steady, even as his throat constricted. He needed these paintings. What he wouldn't do for them. And if she didn't sell them to the museum, what *would* he do for them?

"No," Rebecca said, cutting off his spiraling line of thought. "I want to donate them to the museum. No money necessary. Just promise me you'll put them all on display as soon as you can."

All of the tension that had seized the curator's muscles now melted away like they were part of that odd painting with the crying child.

"That's incredibly generous of you!" the curator blurted out. He could weep. "We will definitely put these on display. In fact, I'm going to want to put on a special exhibition." He waved his hands in the air. 'Isidoro Cervantes: Rediscovered and Reborn!' Maybe we could make it a traveling exhibition. International! Wouldn't that be wonderful? I would love for these paintings to help revive an interest in a painter who has been undeservedly forgotten."

"That would be amazing," Rebecca said, her voice thick with what could only be emotion. "I'm ecstatic that I could be part of something as monumental as this. Picture all the aspiring artists out there who will get to see this spectacular artwork. Just think of how inspired they will be as they lay eyes on things once forgotten but now remembered."

"My thoughts exactly!" the curator exclaimed.

Rebecca Espinoza leaned toward him. Had her eyes flashed again just now?

"Yes, just think of all the things they will imagine."

AUTHOR'S NOTE

Each chapter title, as well as the prologue and epilogue titles, are riffs on the titles of artwork that I carefully selected to represent each segment. I encourage the reader to look up the artwork for their own consideration and appreciation.

Prologue: At Damnation's Gate
At Eternity's Gate
by Vincent van Gogh, 1890

Chapter One: The Great Red Fiend and the Girl Clothed with the Sun
The Great Red Dragon and the Woman Clothed with the Sun
by William Blake, 1805

Chapter Two: Superstition
Apparition
by Adolf Hirémy-Hirschl, date unknown

Chapter Three: House of Shadows
Realm of Shadows
by Joseph Vargo, 2000

Chapter Four: Disturbing Existence
Disturbing Presence
by Remedios Varo, 1959

Chapter Five: Every Night Inspiration Visits Us
Every Night a Dream Visits Us
by Alfred Kubin, 1900

Chapter Six: Visión Fantasmala
Visión Fantasmal
by Francisco Goya, 1797

Chapter Seven: Greyed-Hair Rainbow
Greyed Rainbow
by Jackson Pollock, 1953

Chapter Eight: Silence Everywhere
Silence
by Henry Fuseli, 1801

Chapter Nine: The Re-correction of Chris
The Resurrection of Christ
by Noel Coypel, 1700

Chapter Ten: Figure with Roots
Figure with Meat
by Francis Bacon, 1954

Chapter Eleven: The Painter and the Puppet
The Woman and the Puppet
by Ángel Zárraga, 1909

Chapter Twelve: The Great Day of His Masterpiece
The Great Day of His Wrath
by John Martin, 1853

Epilogue: Vanitas Still Life Goes On
Vanitas Still Life
by Phillippe de Champaigne, 1671

ACKNOWLEDGMENTS

None of my work would be possible without my wife, Erin. Not only does she encourage me with every story I create, she also is the first to wield the red pen when it comes to my first drafts. Megan M Davies-Ostrom and Robert P. Ottone deserve much gratitude for their encouragement and invaluable feedback that helped steer this story in the right direction. The Horror Writers Association and the fellow writers I've befriended through the organization are always dependable when you need guidance, community, and cheerleaders. And finally, I want to give many, many thanks to Michael Dolan and WRDS for picking up *Rootfingers* and giving it a fantastic home to haunt.

S. Alessandro Martinez is a Bram Stoker Award® - nominated author of Mexican and Spanish descent, avid gamer, bat fancier, and necromancer enthusiast who writes horror and fantasy for adults and children. *Rootfingers* is his first book for Winding Road Stories.

www.ingramcontent.com/pod-product-compliance
Lightning Source LLC
Chambersburg PA
CBHW031058310726
48969CB00007B/2335